Queen's Landing

Copyright © 2023 Robert W. Moore

All rights reserved.

No part of this publication may be reproduced, stored in a retrieval system, or transmitted in any form or by any means, electronic, mechanical, photocopying, recording, or otherwise, without permission of the author.

Disclaimer: The title of this book is used under parody only and is in no way affiliated with or intended to infringe upon the subject matter of A Game of Thrones by George R.R Martin or its televised series.

Contributors:

Miss Josh Emmett
Elissa Gooden
Briana M. Miles
SnowRainStella
Amy Tracy

The Servant's Acknowledgments

Thanks to Neil Wight, my editor and part-time servant to the queen. I promise she'll be nicer to you. Well, I can't make promises she won't keep. Kodi misses you and wants you to know he's a very gooboi.

Thank you to to all of Shorty and Kodi's followers, especially those of you from day one. You have given joy and community to this shy, introverted cat dad. A big thanks to the Patreon and YouTube subscribers; without your support I might not have kept going. To the writers who contributed works for this book: your creativity is amazing and humbling. I'm glad you found inspiration in these funny characters as I have and submitted these wonderful poems and stories.

To my kitties: every day you teach me and still me and offer what we human morons consistently forget: the ability to live completely in the moment. And I'm the luckiest person in the world to share these incredible moments with you. Thank you for rescuing me.

Finally, to Bryan, the other servant and amazing cat dad: how a person treats animals says everything about them. And you are the kindest, gentlest, most empathetic person I know. Thank you for being the one to suggest going to the shelter all those years ago.

Table of Contents

The Book of Shorty 1

Chapter 1 5

Chapter 2 25

Chapter 3 43

Chapter 4 59

Chapter 5 67

Chapter 6 75

Chapter 7 103

Chapter 8 105

The Book of Kodi 115

The Book of Fur Fiction 117

   Realization of The Royal Queen ... 119

   Three Thoughts of One Activity ... 126

   Hiss Me Deadly 129

   Me, Your Majestic Highness 132

   Queen and the Hell Gate 135

   The Fool's Folly 149

The Book of Shorty

In my stars I am above thee; but be not afraid of greatness: some are born great, some achieve greatness, and some have greatness thrust upon 'em.

- William Shakespeare, *Twelfth Night*
  or
- Queen Shoshobeans, *Every Night*

Chapter 1

Night falls. The commotion of the day softens into the pause between breaths. My queendom calms, the castle quiets, the candles, consumed. A chill creeps across the land and crosses my fuzzy paw like a sandpaper tongue on supple, salty, furless skin. Soothing.

The servants hath retreated to their sleeping quarters, seemingly satisfied, for some reason, with the completion of their duties. Dimwits. The palace is putrid, slovenly, a holy mess of a rat's nest. I don't exaggerate, a large rat moved in quite some time ago and found the place so fetid it never left it.

But alas, the discord fades as dark replaces day. Before me, a long, dark hallway stretches further and darker into the night. Not a speck of sneaky sun can shine into this abyss yet I see more because of this. 'Tis within the fresh shroud of shade and stillness that I wake beyond wakefulness. I am the watcher of the halls, after all. And some must watch, while some Dimwits must sleep. And as the castle nestles into a slumber of ominous creaks and mournful moans, 'tis my duty to guard all within my home. If I had a choice, perhaps I too could drift listlessly into blissful repose to prepare for the morrow's full agenda of nappings. But then I'd have to depend solely on the humans for defence through the night. We'd surely be dead by dawn. Dimwits.

No, this is my time, with the steel of my gaze and my swords on the ready. So begins the Night Watch.

Sacrifice.

No one knows the lengths I go to sacrifice all for them. Each could be slain through the night if 'twere not for my persistent patrol. The Shadow Demons, for example, would surely bring death to us all if I didn't bat them away with an imperious *tap-tap*. The ghosts, they cackle and raise my hackles in knowing that something comes wicked this way. I spy them now, the almost imperceptible phantoms that frolic through the front room. Take that! *tap-tap*. And that! *tap-tap*. They are vanquished, and I am again victorious. "Rest ye weary lot," I call out to my coward wards sleeping peacefully, "for thine enemy lies vanquished, and all is good."

Indeed, rowdy intruders threaten our house nightly. Not to mention that spiteful sprite perched halfway up the back wall ready to attack at any moment. O, how it mocks me, laughing at my attempts to smack it into oblivion as it remains, unmoved, night after night, taunting me. "It's just a mark on the wall, a mere spot," the servants tell me repeatedly. But I know better, this cunning marauder that must be banished. I jump at it now, straining to scratch at the surface just beneath it, the revolting gnat just out of reach, and demand its surrender. "Out, damn'd spot! Out, I say!" The shriek of my swords against the wall pierces the night air warning all that a Mad Queen bubbles just beneath a furry surface. I jump and I jerk and I clamour and claw until I'm certain I've scared it into submission. A servant hollers, "Huzzah!" in appreciation from their sleeping quarters, and I am pleased.

I march onward through the corridor, into the darkness, cutting through the stillness like a fang into flesh. And though she be but little, she is fierce!

Responsibility.

I've not slept a wink this restless night. The humans have wasted precious days redecorating the castle and have moved all my couches and napping furniture into a mass of disarray. While I take account of ensuring my home be as uninviting as possible to visitors, what with their repulsive smells and soiled, seeking mitts, methinks this a tad extreme. Dimwits.

They are oblivious to the demons their mess hath invited. Prithee, why hast thou plunged the populace into chaos? Why so much dithering hither and thither throughout the day? Let every cat be master of their time and none would whither a whisker in wont of a disorganized dwelling.

And what's this? An outrageousness! My eyes doth see but they can't believe! Is this a dagger which I see before me? Worse, a closed door! O, what contemptuous foes would wage such hideous forces 'gainst their compassionate queen. 'Tis an affront! An assault! An offence to my very preeminence! I charge at the despicable door now, heaving my full - but still very slight, mind you - weight against its blockade swinging my steel like a savage brigade.

"Once more unto the breach, my swords!" I scrape and scratch the deeds of death into the door, marking and marring the detestable wood. I pause, hearing a cry in the night. A call! A caterwaul? 'Twas nothing at all! I resume my strike with a left over right and pummel the obstacle with all of my might. "O, that I could see what sights unseen beyond this rampart that I didn't permit!" My voice rises and roars like an angel of war to cast out this most ghastly indignity and -

"O, human!" My swordsmanship successfully knocked down the gate to reveal a servant before me, their sleeping quarters just beyond. "Ahoy hoy. What sayeth thou?" The human proceeds to offer exuberant acclamations and most definitely *huzzahs* for alerting them to the closed door. Actually, they're quite vehement about it, dear soul.

"Don't mention it, peasant. Your queen thanks you for your labour and loyalty. Fare thee well." I nose the air with a trill denoting safety which comforts the buffoon, and they retreat graciously, albeit leaden-footed, back to their bed. Dimwit. I can now continue the perimeter-check unabated. Though somewhat unsatiated. Onward to satiate and then to siege!

But how, pray tell, how can one properly watch over the house in its sloppy state? Every corner has changed, every piece rearranged. Battlements have been erected to various heights haphazardly throughout the castle yet my cursed dainty limbs prevent me from ascending them for proper surveillance. The scrawny Simpleton - the aforementioned large rat that squatted its spotted butt here and never departed - scales them with ease with nary a clue of what to do. Even my carpeted throne is sullied and strewn with debris! Alas, a better defence, thence, is made from the floor for who knows what hides in this mercurial maze. So many new corridors to investigate, enemy hidings to infiltrate, an ever-shifting landscape to navigate. One might question me for not posting a trusted soldier to guard the castle rather than taking it upon myself. Find me such a worthy paladin within my keep and I'll find you a dog that doesn't reek of a hundred hairballs retched into a dirty litter box on a steaming hot day. Can't be done.

Empathy.

Dull though they may be, my wards are endearing little chattels, earnest in their attempts to appease their queen. They regularly offer gifts and a warm place to rest my head, heavy from the crown. Though I must be quite stern with them, they keep the dining schedule timely and are attentive to my poopsies. They even manage to scratch the hard-to-reach place just behind my ears that I can't quite access. Dainty limbs, you see. And indeed, 'tis amusing to hear them mumble inanities as they struggle with communication. I've managed to decipher a few idioms from their crude tongue, most notably *"treat-treats"* and *"foooood"* both spoken with an odd, rising pitch that is entirely annoying but nonetheless recognizable and ultimately rewarding. I'm learning to mimic their simple speech that we may someday better communicate, though I confess my *"foooood"* sounds more like *"prrbbtt"* and they respond only by cooing and laughing maniacally until our exchange descends into some warped form of quid pro quo. Dimwits. I've tried to teach them to use their eyes and ears to communicate - should we venture out on a hunt together, that vacuous, booming maw of theirs would surely be our downfall - but they stare at me like idiots staring into the sun and with as much comprehension.

Ah, my simple servants. They seek counsel constantly and I pity their dependence. They keep asking me who a good girl is like a phonograph that keeps skipping and repeating itself. "Who's a good girl? Who's a good girl? Who's a good girl?" How should a queen have any information on the common townspeople beyond the castle, and why do they want to know? Whether they be good or bad, they'd avoid coming here if they know what's good for them.

They oft wonder aloud where their coins have gone when they could simply bend the knee and see how skillfully I've strewn them beneath the treasury. I believe they call it a cabinet, a heavy thing of planks and metal that is the safest spot for coins, buttons, and jewelry confiscated from guests as a penance for annoying me. Thankfully, my treasury remains undisturbed for it's the only piece of furniture that hasn't been moved as of late. Dimwits.

They also constantly request the identity of the miscreant who vomits occasionally on the rug, as if a queen would ever admit to such a transgression. But honestly who wove that thing anyway? Deserves to be vomited on if you ask me. Oh right, they did ask me. Well, it's neither here nor there. But if I had to do it, I'd do it there, not here.

But I sympathize with the disadvantaged so I disregard their musings. It's not their fault they were born limited in so many ways, nor is it mine should I feel the need to test their limits over and over and over again. All the better to understand them, you see. For example, I've determined that their vision is compromised at night, and stepping in front of them as they stumble to the water chamber mid-slumber is strictly to teach them better balance and to not be so stupid. It's not working but I don't stop trying. The fact that it also provides ample entertainment to me is simply good fortune. Thus, while their brains are grossly stunted, they are satisfactory in attending my needs and amusing to have around, so 'tis my duty to both protect and suffer the fools.

Leadership.

To be a great leader, one must be diligent in keeping the forces ready to battle oncoming foes; I can't very well lead an attack with an unprepared army no matter how dense they may be. Therefore, a nightly drill is necessary that we may form our defence as a coordinated force.

But then, something is telling me it's now too late for a test. I sense the light of night beginning to change, a hum of hounds in the distance, a town rubbing the fog from its sleepy street eyes. Morning is imminent. I've been distracted by deliberating on my duties. And now an attack is coming and the servants are vulnerable. I can feel my pupils widen, straining to see the perils before me. The dark is darkening and about to break, the dawn dragon inhaling and about to wreak havoc and fire on all of us lest we safeguard the castle! The flying vermin outside could even start chirping any second! Then where will we be? Defenceless. We must make a stand post haste. Wait! Was that a chirp I just heard? Was it a beep? Do I know the difference? Yes! Surely it was! Either and or! Cannon to the right of me! Cannon to the left of me! Cannon in front of me, volley'd and chirp'd! Ready or not, I must lead the troops into battle.

"Awaken, ye lot!" My rallying call stabs through the silent, starless night. "A malevolent dragon threatens to permeate these walls and diurnal creatures will surely arise and pull us asunder. Awaken, I say!"

No response. Nothing.

"Hear ye, hear ye! Your queen commands thee! Join me at the front lines to defend the castle!" Silence. Insolence? Insanity! Perhaps they are vanquished. Yes. 'Tis the only explanation for my abandonment. The Dimwits are dead, distinguished by demons unknown. 'Tis I who have failed. I alone possessed the skill to protect the house, and though I stood steadfast in my duty, my army has fallen. An arrogant chirp echoes faintly in the distance. Could still be a beep. The township outside wakes and readies its forces without my permission nor preparation.

"O spiteful world, woe is *meeee*," I exclaim. "Why hast thou forsaken *MEEE? OOOHHH!*" I am inconsolable as I cry into a chasm of uncertainty. Can I go on? Where will my next apprehensive steps lead? Deserted by my people, I am left to fend for myself in these dark times. I pace the corridor, defeated.

I must check the rations for who knows how long I have to endure this desolate journey on my own. No matter. I myself am best when least in company, if not for the part about opposable thumbs. Ah, that reminds me. But what's this? My supplies are depleted. The food dish is nearly half empty. Seems I've only enough provisions to last until my interest wanes which could be any second now. The life in the lap of luxury as I have known surrounded by servants is over, gone, destroyed. I am undone. I continue down the corridor to relish in what moments of darkness remain.

The castle is quiet, conquered. In all of existence, it has never been so quiet, so absent of all that hath given me joy and comfort. All lives lost yet I alone remain. But for how long? The anxiety creeps along my spine and brings a tremble, a twitch. Wait! What's this? What do I see before me? An orb? A ghost! No, 'tis my Beautiful Tail! Wrought with worry, my Beautiful Tail flits this way and that. I pause to groom my Beautiful Tail and it feels comforting, calming, like a salve to the wound that is my despair. *O, my Beautiful Tail, we have only each other now. I am so grateful to have you for though my servants were doting, at least ye are nice to look at.* Wait! This must be what they want, the demons who've slain my staff. They want my Beautiful Tail! They are keen at night, but dexterous by day, and dawn doth approacheth! I groom my Beautiful Tail quicker, faster, with vigour and vim. I've so little time to groom my Beautiful Tail! They can't get it. I won't allow it. I'll get it first! I twist around and around. My determination is as fierce as my tail is beautiful. I've got it! I've got my tail! And it... hurts. *OUCH!* My Beautiful Tail recoils and breaks free from my grasp. But wait, Beautiful Tail, I have to protect you. Get back here. Hold still! There you are. *OUCH!*

What's that? A noise? Down the hall? In my head? In my stead! I let go of my Beautiful Tail. The raid is upon us. Upon me! I shan't let the house fall. My battle cry is fierce and powerful as it thunders through the castle halls. "I am *QUEEEEN!* Here me *NEOOOOWWW!*"

I hear a call in the distance. A stirring. A whirring? A voice! Could it be? Yes! A servant's voice! O, joyous moment. It's not too late after all. I pummel back down the corridor, buoyed by the evidence that my troops still live, to lead the onslaught against the impending morn and its doomsday, dragon's eye sun. "This is my HOUSE! This is where we fight! This is where they die!" I sound my barbaric yawp over the roofs of the world, a warning to the dawn that threatens to invade at any instant. The servants, apparently revived and well and inspired by my courage, have finally joined my chorus to defend these walls. "Huzzah! Huzzah," is what I'm certain they are shouting from their chamber in pure admiration of their queen. We continue back and forth, my staff and I, until we are roaring in a frightening unison to ward off the attack.

I run to the window to confront her head on, my ultimate foe, the dreaded dragon. I must be strong. I must also have fire in my eyes when I face it. A daring twinkle of flames flicker arrogantly across the fading night sky. Its sinister rise begins. To move is to stir, and to be valiant is to stand; I shan't be moved for I am queen of this land!

The surly sun, you see, brings forth an array of cacophonous creatures from its daylight dimension, determined to - dare I say it aloud - disturb my naps! Aye, 'tis most egregious to disturbeth the nappeth of the catteth with the chatter and clatter and busyness that brightness brings. And with my castle rearranged, the Dimwits have laid bare the perfect scenario for the onslaught of Shadow Demons throughout the wretched day, the vanquishing of which shall steal precious time from my royal naps. The world may fall this very day!

And so I sit and I stare and I dare the rising to transpire. And sometimes that dragon looks right into you, right into your eyes. The thing about a dragon is it's got lifeless eyes and you don't know it's even shining until it shines onto you! O, the power it has to rain fire onto all of us! But it knows not the power I yield for only I can peer right back. As it grows brighter, I am unmoved, my eyes shrinking to mere slits. Most must turn away but not I. 'Tis up to me, Queen Shorty Shoshobeans, First of Her Name and Ruler of this Land to stand steadfast against the deceitful day. All my means are sane, though my motive and my object may be mad. I stare unblinkingly into the dragon's heart. 'Tis the only way to be sure that all the world will be in love with night and pay no worship to the garish sun.

One must show strength as it rises, to call on the ancestors, to sing the song of our people, to deny that we will go quietly with the night, to vanish without a fight! "YOU SHALL NOT PASS!" My roar meets the dragon's fire head on as it burns a clear path over the town below, hurdling to the windows of my castle where I stand, threatening to incinerate us all if I am to show an ounce of fear. There it stands by a quarter, now a half, now at full staff! The open eye of the hydra now on the horizon and I the immovable ruler of this dimension. "Rise, dear dragon, for I allow thee to rise. Breathe, for I command thee to breathe. But no speck of this land, no cat, vermin or human shall be singed by thy surly scowl." But if she takes a dog or two, that wouldn't be the worst thing.

And it is done. My sheer ferocity hath cut the strength of the dragon's fire to a muted warm, and no harm has befallen us on this day. The world bears witness to my absolute greatness for I've bested the beast into submission.

"Well done, my people," I sing out. "Fear no more the fire. We have overcome a worthy adversary yet again. Let us celebrate in song! MEOOOWWW!!!" O, excellent! A ward now feels safe to venture out of their sleeping chamber and is joining me as we run about the grounds, drunk with victory. Yes, servant, yes, run this way and that in this maze thou hast created! What fun as they try to match my every turn. But they are heavy-footed and slack-limbed whilst I am nimble and quick and, oops, not so nimble I'm afraid, but the servants shouldn't have left that glass in the middle of the table directly in my path. I am the first to the end of the hall and back and around again. They keep trying to catch up, all the while shouting, and I am most certain of this now, "HUZZAH, HUZZAH!" Oh, my funny, feeble-minded folk, you amuse me so.

The servant, pleased with assisting my courtly calisthenics, hath provided provisions for my post-exercise feast and retired once again to their chambers. I shall wake them again with thanks and praise shortly, but first, a quick bite, and an assessment of the premises.

The gate is secure. The walls are intact. The palace, though a frightful shambles, houses no intruders. None shall know the full extent of my great victory. No matter. When the blast of war blows, none can imitate the action of the tiger. In peace there's nothing so becomes a cat as modest stillness and humility. But I am no mere cat.

I am Queen.

The Simpleton watches from on high atop a shoddily-erected battlement like a half-baked black and white gargoyle. I nearly succeeded in forgetting its existence. I nose the air in the dope's direction. *Some help you were in the battle, you mashed-up Oreo rugrat!* It was probably nestled betwixt the servants whilst they slept, so needy it is for human connection. *You're an affront to felinekind!* I avoid direct eye contact lest it think me interested in, ugh, playing. But I know it's watching, so I squint my eyes and flatten my ears, more out of habit than an actual communiqué; the dolt can't decode which parts of its body are its own lest interpret observable language. I ignore its attention-seeking ear-flittings and head to the arrow-slits of the curtain wall.

Morning fully breaks. From my tower several stories high, I see the commoners below, the fluffy-tailed rodents skittering atop the town's dwellings, shiny, noisy elephants rumbling past, the obnoxious flying rats keeping their distance. The dragon maintains her distance with a humbled eye hovering in the sky. But I am ruler of this domain and I am satisfied that all the day's creatures have fallen in line under my powerful gaze.

Because I am a benevolent ruler, I announce to my house that all is well and serenade them with song. Music is the food of love, after all, and I know how much the servants enjoy feeling loved by the vocal stylings of their queen in the early morn. Their appreciation comes immediate and emphatic from the sleeping quarters - "Huzzah, My Queen, HUZZAH!" - and that is absolutely what they're saying now I'm sure of it, and it is good. Well, not all good; the servants picked a fine day to sleep in for this palace *could use some servanting!* More huzzahs, most definitely, in response.

My queendom is prosperous and I look forward to extending my royal dominion. But for now I shall lay on my back and allow the defeated sun to warm my full, fuzzy belly. Perhaps I can lull an errant hand there for a sacrifice later, and it shall be amusing.

Chapter 2

I am awoken by a flurry of sound from a furry mound. The Simpleton! It's wailing away about everything and nothing. *Get thee away!* I swat at the bothersome blight to keep its distance. Seems it was spooked by some goings-on of the servants and misplaced itself next to me. *How dare you interrupt my nap you spotted scoundrel!* It's turned its hollow head away, probably hoping I'm too tired to retaliate. *You're right, but you're still stupid!*

I roll onto my back to rest my tired limbs and weary soul just a bit longer. O, to be human and have nary a care in the world besides stuffing their faces and staring blankly at a shimmering screen. Freedom from wit frees the shackles of thought for the humans have not a thought to be thunk!

Indeed, Your Queen doth suffer great adversity in this sea of troubles. Between the Night Watch, caring for the servants, and admonishing the court jester who never knows when to jest and when to leave me the hell alone, I've so much to deal with it's ofttimes too much. Plus, the castle's concrete floor is hard on my feetsies. *A loft*, as our dwelling is so named by the servants, with a floor of stone most unbecoming of a queen's palace. I've had to grow extra fur on my feetsies just to get some cushioning beneath them! Dimwits.

I stretch and let a giant sigh flow through my heavy limbs. I can't move, my limbs feel so heavy. They're as concrete as this damned floor. Nevertheless. Though floors and wars be troublesome, I must escape to slumber's warm embrace and meet what queenly dreams may come. The mastery of lethargy is the most glorious of the gifts bestowed on the feline, you know. Humans, however, view sleep as a chore. And like most of their duties, they don't do it well.

I'll let you in on a secret, dear reader, for the bounds of my benevolence are not limited to permitting peasantly existence, but they extend to the effort of expanding simple minds no matter how pointless a venture. And if ye are of the furless bipedal varietal, then I do indeed pity thy chances for achievement. We felines began domesticating humans because we took note of their aimless ambling and strange predilection for stacking stones which proved very useful in allowing us to ascend great heights and look down on every living thing. But we thought humans needed a greater purpose, a goal to validate such mundane lives. A life of servitude to the felis catus seemed the least we could do if only to give thee a reason to wake in the morning.

Yes, Your Queen believes humans to possess a morsel of potential, despite what the entirety of the animal kingdom claims. No, no, I think ye are more than just "oppressive meat bags," the colloquial term for humans on which every sentient animal agrees. Well, except for dogs. Dogs think you're wonderful. For a creature equally excited by food, fetch, and feces, that's not saying much.

Now, where was I? *Yawwwn.* Oh right, the sumptuous snack of snoozing, the delicious din-din of dozing. If sleep be the main course in this great feast then ye are surely famished! O, you poor humans with your tossing and turning and fumbling and farting all the night through. Even after all these eons, you're barely housebroken! 'Tis a wonder we let you in from the barn to share our dwelling, let alone sleep in our beds. But heed Your Queen's words, for they are as close to the divine consciousness as your limited intellect could grasp.

Sleep is not a need, like drinking or eating or sniffing someone's hand before touching them (and really, you should practice the latter a little more often; humans are filthy). No, no. 'Tis a state of being, a constitution. You can't desire to sleep, you have to *be* sleep. Otherwise you'll be too anxious in lacking that for which you are longing. Like a horse passing the day grazing away, the cat continually sips from the trough of tranquility keeping life's sufferings at bay. 'Tis not a source of stress, silly human. The reason the nap is associated with cat is because you can't think of one without thinking of the other, they go together so well. Like the words, human moron. You see how well they go together? You can't possibly separate the two. When two concepts are so complementary, they are linked. And thus, we have "catnap," ergo, we have "human moron." It just makes sense, and this sense is common, and thus it is common sense that cats are good at napping and that humans are morons.

Do you understand now? Humans, for example, don't have to try to be morons, they simply are, and so there's no effort expended in trying to be morons. Therefore, treat sleep like you do being morons. For cats, sleep lies in the nature of being. But for human beings, sorry, human morons, with their impatience, lack of balance, and obsession with closing doors, being human seems quite the burden. So, fare thee well with all of that.

Alas, all this enlightening has left me over-taxed. But if my goodwill results in just the slightest improvement in your mental capacity and your ability to stop kicking us in your sleep, then we'll all be grateful won't we. 'Tis my gift to you, my dear, dull, furless human morons. It's like the old saying, "Do unto others so that they're less stupid." You may ponder the importance of this statement, if possible, whilst I welcome rest's great nourishment.

Queening is hard work, indeed.

...

I am again awoken by a commotion. Woe is me, I am not afforded the luxury to lie untroubled. For trouble is afoot! Or is it apaw? Having humans as one's only companions for so long has me quite confused. *Simpleton will you silence your wailing I'm trying to figure out if it's afoot or apaw!* I cast a quick glare of daggers at the nuisance that is currently warbling for attention. The servants are banging and clanging and barking and charging. O, that I should enjoy a respite from the royal demands of not only caring for and protecting these servants but saving their very lives! And this is the thanks I get. Dimwits.

They're erecting more walls and barriers throughout the grounds. I spy them now swerving and stomping and carrying and dropping. *Must you make such a racket!* I turn my ears sidewise and downward ready to scold them with a scowl. The servants may seem slow but they know exactly what I am saying. Expressing displeasure is an art form mastered by the feline, after all. *And I've plenty to express!* They are now pretending to ignore my protestations. *Yawn.* I shan't get a wink of deserved rest around here. I may as well investigate.

I shake off the sleep and lumber through a maze of barricades to a low wall being erected with large stones. O, they've devolved to Egyptian times! Poor stunted beings. But at least more statues shall be erected in my honour. We've been too easy on humans, they forgot about the importance of basic masonry and monuments. Dimwits.

But these stones are green. And hard, my sword can't but gain purchase against its smooth surface. O, how I do love green for how it matcheth my emerald eyes. Like I'm staring into my very own beauty. Hm.

This green stone smells funny. I rub my cheek along its edge to assume property. *This is mine now, ye lot!* Hm. Still smells funny. Like stale hope and old regret. O yes, dear reader, cats can smell many feelings and intentions. Just one of the many gifts and advantages afforded us over humans, like four legs and composure.

Hope, when a human is eager with anticipation, smells a bit like a ripe, freshly cut honeydew melon, a sweetness that is fragile and fleeting. It's what we felines expect when we bring them gifts of dying rodents for instance. For who doesn't hold the greatest hope when opening the bowels of a gift? Humans, however, haven't yet grasped the art of gratitude for instead of dining on the gift, they toss it away, smelling nothing like the honeydew we had hoped for. Dimwits. The honeydew smell is strongest when the human comes running after hearing a hairball being expelled. Their hope is that the vomit missed the detestable rug. Wrong again, silly human! Always wrong. Maybe someday they'll get the message.

But hope, much like a honeydew, turns rotten if held too long and becomes anger. I know because I once held hope the Simpleton was only visiting. Thus, anger smells of rotten fruit - apples, to be more precise - with acidic overtones and a crisp, caustic finish. One time a small apple somehow slipped beneath the ice box when I was pushing it there, and a fortnight later I couldn't tell if it was the fruit I was smelling or a servant's reaction at having again discovered an allowance left for them in front of the litter box. Perhaps if they cleaned it more regularly, they'd smell less like angry rotten apples and the castle would smell less like my poopsies.

Yes, this strange green stone smells of old honeydew hope, but also regret, which resembles rancid milk that's just begun to curdle. At first you think you can tolerate it but a closer sniff causes a recoil in disgust, much like when I gaze upon the Simpleton. Well, it's either the rank scent of regret or the Simpleton just stinks. One can never know.

By the by, contentment, my favourite scent, is like a plastic bag fresh from the market. I could chew on that all day if the humans weren't fanatical about storing them away like mad chipmunks. I don't jest, I see the pile of plastic bags when they open the cupboard. What are they preparing for, the apocalypse? Too late, I'm surrounded by nonsensical zombies making numbskull decisions.

Another of my favoured scents emanates from, as I've come to understand it, sickness and/or sadness. When a human lays about covered in tapestries and liquid falls from their eyes and noses, while also making god-awful noises, they smell like a freshly opened can of salmon that you can't wait to slurp up until it's all gone. The scent is hypnotic and forces the cat to stay by their side until the human no longer smells of it. The servants think me sympathetic when I attend to their malady when all I really am is hungry.

Right now, I smell dried-up honeydew-hope and rancid milk-regret off this green boulder. I wonder why? Suddenly, a whiff of rotten-apple anger wafts by. A servant's stump whips past and thrashes against my Beautiful Tail. I look up at the towering, disobedient servant. *Such insolence!* They are raising their voice suggesting a sense of urgency while the other one reinforces and stacks the green stones, one on top of the other, with haste. I perceive no impending foe so I don't know what all the anger and fuss of defence is for. After all, 'twas I who saved the castle and all who reside within this very morn! I clean my Beautiful Tail fervently to rid it of the rotten apple scent left by the insubordinate underling. I'll steer clear of them for now until they smell better. I turn back to the green stone which stands just taller than I and twice my length, and set my front paws on the top edge to peek above its crest.

What's this? The rectangular stone is hollow, empty! It even slips a bit on the cursed concrete floor it's so slight. Some buttress this would be against a bombardment. Dimwits. I take several small inhalations from the cavity of the hollow stone to taste the rancid milk, the stale melon, and now a hint of old sneakers which could be nostalgia or old sneakers.

O, wait! This stone isn't for war defence. 'Tis a green box, a sturdy thing, a gift for their queen! And better, a much used box from various places yonder! I leap happily into my new acquirement, realizing it to be made of a hard plastic, a superb smell tainted with human encumbrances. I roll about to lend my present a more pleasing scent. What rapturous sounds my swords make in this hard hollow shell. Scratching in this corner sounds like this: *scratch-scratch-scratch.* I wonder what it sounds like in that corner? I turn round in one swift motion to try and it sounds like this: *scratch-scratch-scratch.* Wondrous! I wonder if the result has changed in the previous corner? I flip over swiftly and try again. s*cratch-scratch-scratch.* Joyous event, it sounds anew! I wonder how deep my new hovel delves? I scratch at its floor, sliding and scraping the surface in a symphony of sound. Try as I may, the floor doesn't give way, but dismayed I am not! *scratch-scratch-scratch.* A tornado of loose fur arises from my domain as I skillfully shuffle off my dead-ends and knots in a beauty regimen that may appear as if I am simply hurling myself violently side to side but is actually quite dignified.

My spa day is interrupted by a thump against my new favourite procurement and I look up at the source. I see a hideous, blotchy patchwork of mayhem staring down upon me. The Simpleton! It dares try to invade my sanctuary? O, how that face offends me. It's like a mad scientist was attempting to create an onyx feline beauty like myself when a raving white Labrador jumped in at the last second and out popped this one. It looks like a walking stuffed Rorschach test reject.

"HISS! I banish thee, ignorant encroacher!" It raises its muddy paw to swat but I am first with a deft left to the noggin. "HISS! HA! You are no match for me, sullen Simpleton. Be gone!" It retreats and sulks away, then pauses to look back. *Further!* I scream with my narrowed eyes, my ears sidewise.

This fort is mine. Enemies be warned. I peer just over the edge of my prize to spy any and all foes and remain absolutely still. Ears, flattened. Eyes, slits. Stomach, grumbling. It's been at least several minutes since my last meal. I must make furtive attempt through the battlefield to obtain more provisions lest I begin to waste away.

But now there is crashing all around me. Explosions. Defiances! An uprising? A mutiny! Yes, my army of ingrates wants not a moment of peace for their too-compassionate queen. They've turned against me! No matter. I am protected within my magical green stone. I am the the very example of strength and fortitude. I am invisible. I am invincible. My fortress, impenetrable. No one can even touch me or, *BAHHH!* What's this? A strike on my Beautiful Tail! I twist around to see the Simpleton batting at my Beautiful Tail whipping to and fro in a fury. My Beautiful Tail has a mind of her own, you see; I have no more control over her than I do the deceptive Simpleton. "Scat, you stunned skunk!" I let forth a barrage of insults as fatal as my blows. It retreats yet I still see its feets on my stone's precipice, a persistent paw with sheathed claws. "This is no time to play, you demented dalmation! We are under attack!" The Simpleton knows not the portent of the current events. This mutiny could surely result in the world's complete destruction, or at the very least a delayed nap! Then where would we be. Napless? I can't bring myself to imagine it.

    The Simpleton seems to have understood and resigned its game, though it's more likely a servant drew near and it was afraid of being called a "bad boy." Tsk tsk. It seems more keen on appeasing our servants than the other way around. Hasn't quite caught on yet to the hierarchy of this land. O, there's an attendant now longing to attend to me. But they can't see me, cloaked as I am within my magical fortress. "I say, my good servant," I trill with a rising intonation of which they are so fond, revealing my location within the deep bowels of the green box. "Have you come to offer me a gift? A treat-treat perhaps."

They're looming tall over me and requesting information. No, they're suggesting I do something. *Well, human, are you going to just stand there or give me fooood? Prrbbtt?* No, it seems they simply want to praise me, to thank their queen for all my hard work through the Night Watch and for bringing such beauty to their pitiful existence. I nudge my nose in the air and trill again. "Yes, indeed, praise be to me, dutiful ward. That will be all." Suddenly their hulking hands descend upon me and yank me from my magical green fortress before hurling me down to the damned concrete floor in a helpless heap. Well, actually they placed me down quite gently, but still, the audacity!

I am dumbfounded by the defiance. O, what treatment I endure, the torture I must take. The giant's foot is within reach so I give it a punitive smack. *That will teach you!* I flit my right ear to advise against further breaches of conduct. They begin to bark at me while the other human moron begins placing random objects into my new old green fort. I circle around the grunting servant to investigate and jump back into my sanctuary. What's this? They're stocking my box with books, writing utensils, random wires, and their second-skin cloth wraps. "No, no, no, silly. I don't require any of these hindrances in my hideaway," I trill at the servant. "Remove all but the wires which I will enjoy chewing on. And the clothing which I will enjoy lying on. In fact, throw them in the drying mechanism as I'll prefer them warm."

"Queen Shorty, no finer feline has ever graced this world nor ever will," the servant hails down to me. "You deserve all good things and more." Regardless of the accolades, I am once again yanked from my fort and tossed to the floor. Again, they were actually rather nice about it, but still, the impudence!

So be it. This mindless mutiny can carry on without a queen to overthrow nor throw around. Too much spouting and squawking anyway. My next nap has been needlessly preempted by such buffoonery that I find myself quite flummoxed indeed. Calm now, Beautiful Tail. The longer you lash about the more likely you are to be stepped on by one of the stumbling slaves. Dimwits.

I spy the Simpleton staring at me from the servant's sleeping quarters. Seems it has had enough as well. *That's the best idea you've had all day*. And probably the only idea, the brainless dolt. I flit my left ear and saunter through to take refuge beneath the bed to wait out the storm. I let out a low grumble whilst walking past, a warning shot to the Simpleton to avoid any, ugh, snuggling, during nap time. It's hard to tell if there's an inkling of understanding in that thick noggin. With eyes that lazy it could be simultaneously looking at me and enthralled by a piece of dust floating by. Idiot.

Regardless, 'tis time for a much-needed nap. I tune out the chaos beyond the quarters and begin the royal bath. To sink into a soothing sleep, I recite my favoured prose I call 'A Lion's Lullaby.'

O'er the hem and 'neath the bed
I slink to rest my weary head
If something stirs and I should wake
The Simpleton's last breath I'll take.

'Tis just a little poem I wrote to calm the nerves and slip into sleep whenever the humans are restless. I'd repeat it to the Simpleton if *it could tear its face away from its crotch for one second!* My silent scolding somehow interrupts its bathing and it looks up at me, both legs in the air, its head low, ready to dive back in.

It looks like a splayed ampersand. *Yes, you, you crass cretin, I need my sleep so you best keep quiet!* It resumes the base ritual, seemingly unbothered, but my message was received. I curl in a circle and sigh with relief. I need my beauty sleep. I feel a whisp against my whiskers. Ah, yes, my Beautiful Tail also needs her beauty sleep! Yes, Beautiful Tail, *lick lick*, you may also rest and awaken with rejuvenated beauty, *lick lick*. I lift my hind leg to aid the cleaning process. I said it was crass, I didn't say it didn't get the job done.

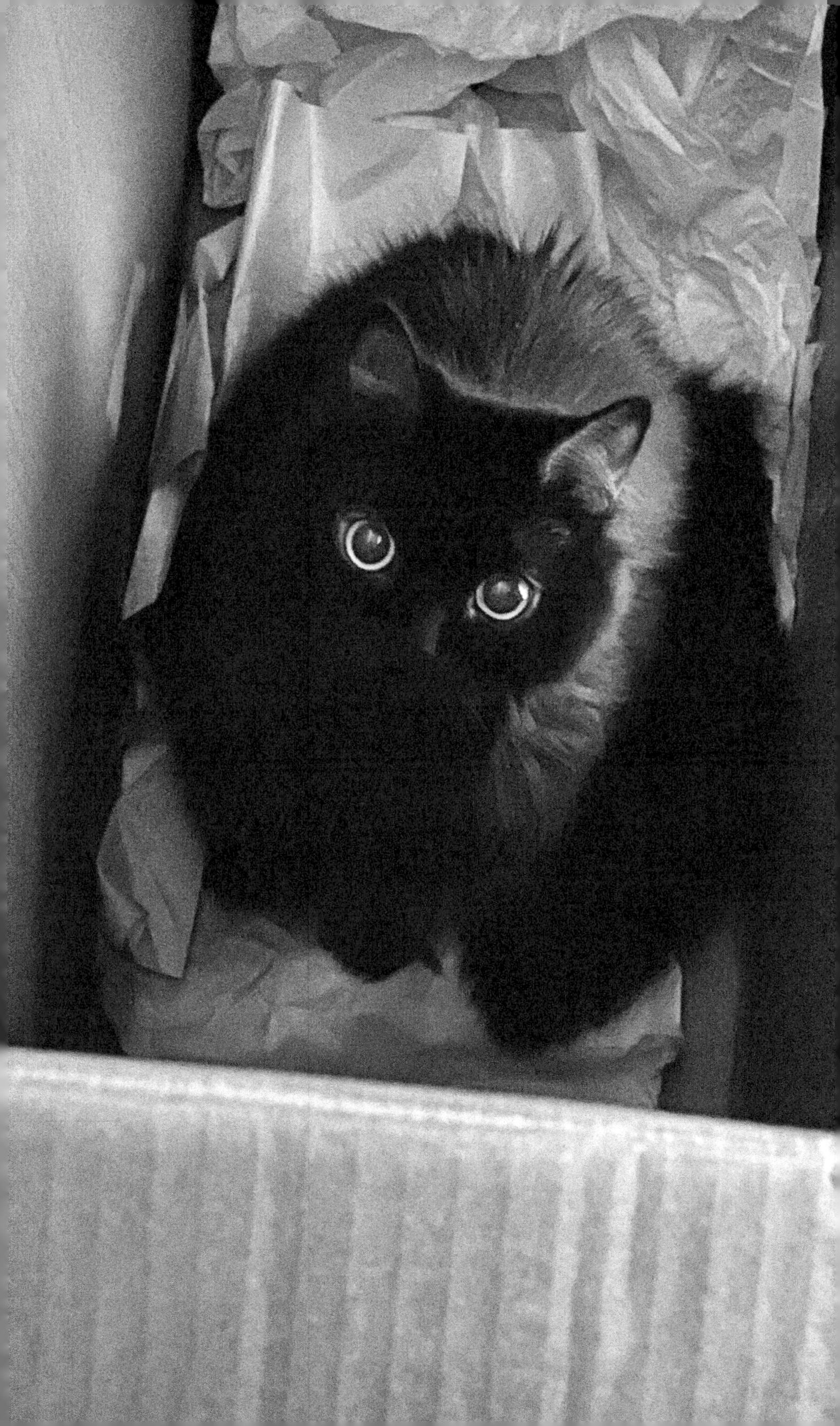

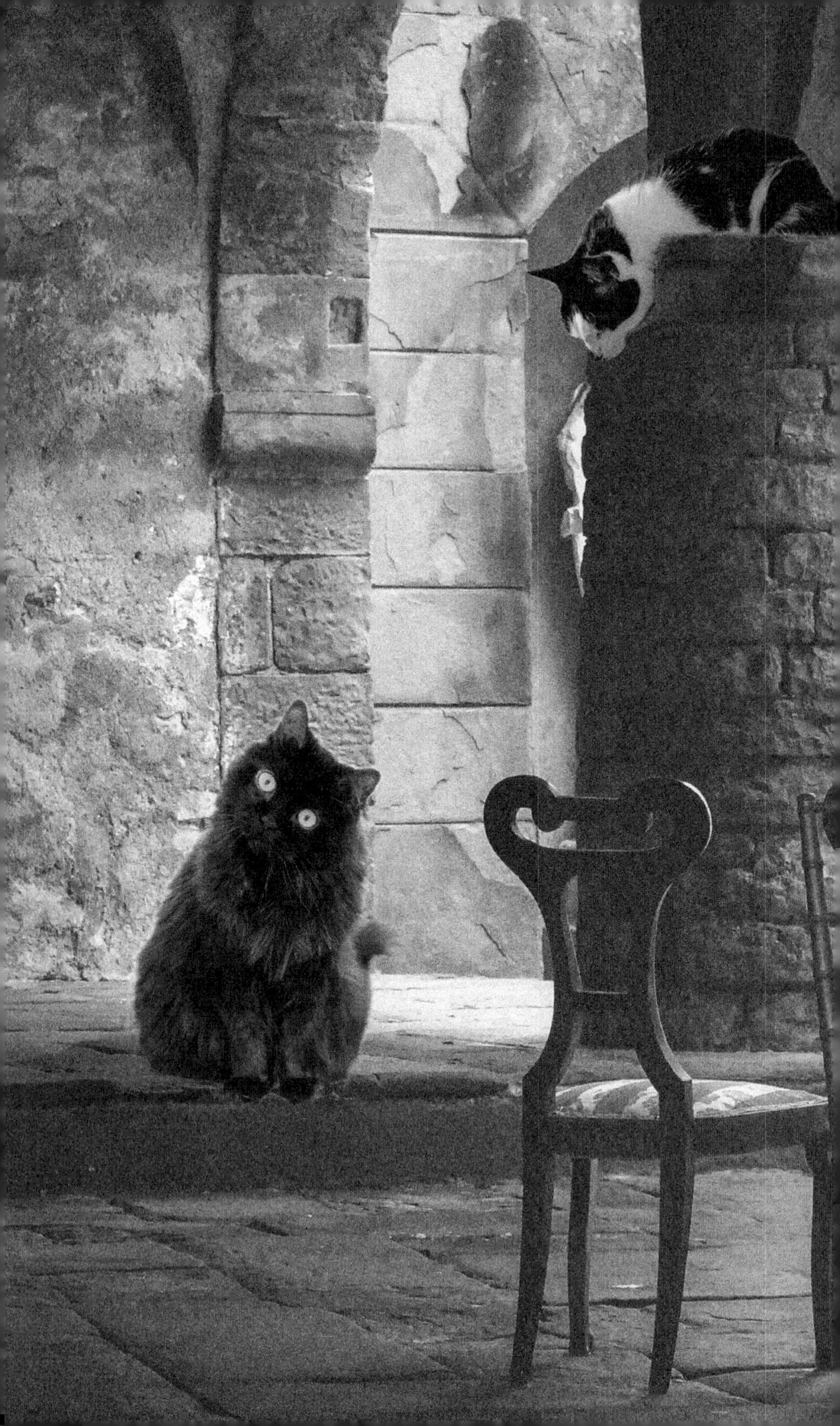

Chapter 3

I am roused by a loud racket just beyond the refuge of the bed. I know not what the servants are up to, though I'm certain it's no good. O, but I am way too comfortable to investigate, the folds of my luxurious fur so like a loving warm embrace. My heavens, I am but a wondrous gift to myself. I sigh and feel overwhelmed with gratitude. *Thank me, thank me for all I do to enhance my grand existence. Thank me.* Gratitude, after all, is the key to happiness, and no one is more grateful to have me in their life as I.

Indeed, despite the rumblings beyond the ramparts, 'tis safe and warm here under the cover of darkness. Especially warm, in fact. Oddly, even. What's this? I feel a rising and falling of harsh quills against my back, like a repellent porcupine coming to terms with its own unpleasantness. I crane my head to see a black and white lump of a louse. I am warmed not by my surroundings but by the Simpleton itself! It ignored my royal decree to stay a furlong away from me. It's plopped itself here against my back, probably to irritate me, or perhaps out of fear of the chaos just beyond the bed's border. Annoying. Yet warming. It reminds me of the heating apparatus, a soft blanket which radiates a glorious warmth, that only appears on the couch when the human is smelling of salmon and sickness. Would it kill them to get sick a little more often that their queen could be comfortable on a toasty tapestry? On second thought, it might. For now I shall allow the indiscretion as the heat pleases me and pretend the Simpleton is just an inanimate object that happens to be warm. I'm probably not far off. At least it's not bounding about as usual like a rabid fleabag. I nuzzle my nose back into my Beautiful Tail. *O'er the hem and 'neath the bed I slink to rest my ...*

...

Thunder. A storm rages. A battalion approaches. The attack comes from all sides. A million mice march toward me, each of them fuzzy and pink with one black ear, a tattered tail in tow. They're angry, vengeful. No, not mice, much bigger than mice. And not pink, but yellow. Bananas. They've all turned into bananas! Could they be my party favour produce? My dope-filled delicacy? The toy of tonic the humans toss about to delight and intoxicate their queen? The fuzzy bananas grow larger as they draw closer. No, they smell not like catnip, like they usually do, but like rotten apples. Angry rotten apples! I'm besieged by an army of angry, rotten, acidic, apple-scented bananas. My feet are a flurry as I strain to scurry as they stampede toward me, but the floor is a cursed concrete and I can't make headway. The ground quakes, the castle shakes. The sky opens up. Literally. The sky is being carried away to reveal the merciless heavens above as it becomes bright, a light so bright that it singes my Beautiful Tail and now she's burned and emaciated like the Simpleton's sorry stub of a tail! O, what a world, what a world!

But what's this? I open my eyes and am drenched in daylight as my protective mattress floats aloft. What spirits are upon me that possess such skill? O, 'tis the minions maintaining their mess-making. They've carried the bed away. *I'm not done sleeping you obstinate fools! Replace my cover at once!* They pretend not to understand my narrowed eyes but they know very well their crime. Punishment will be swift. *Simpleton, attack!* Where… where's it gone? The

Simpleton's vanished. And after my great sacrifice in allowing it to warm me mid-slumber. I shan't do that fool any more favours. A servant addresses me.

"My Queen, your beauty is as boundless as the sea, my love as deep. Might I petteth thee?" They reach down to me, but I am not placated.

"Human, how dare you touch me!" I hiss. "Here's two swats for a penance." I deliver two warning shots with swords sheathed. Should they try again they will taste my steel. They have retreated. The servants turn to each other to battle. Now's my chance to escape. I've lost several naps and not had a decent day's sleep, I'm not about to engage in a surprise cage match. I leap out of the bed-frame and run for cover, motionless for a moment as my claws can't gain traction on the blasted concrete floor.

I run down the corridor and round the corner. *Oof!* Too much speed on the turn and I slide into the wall. I gain purchase and proceed with haste. *Oof!* Where once was a passage is now a barricade. The maze I mastered not hours ago hath been rearranged yet again. I lower myself close to the ground to avoid detection as I slither like a snake amongst the ruins of my house. Everything is different. Same smells, old smells, new smells, foreign smells. Oh, look, a green stone low enough that I may enter. I place my front paws on it, ready to leap into its safety. But wait! This one isn't hollow at all! 'Tis fully enclosed with a top that is hard and flat. Seems sturdy enough to scale. I lean back on my wee hind legs and spring upward. I ascend its height easily as I am lithe and athletic, a powerful panther ready to pounce, dainty legs and all! And it does offer a higher vantage point which shall aid in my counter attack. I think I can make it now to an even higher level, a nearby tower just less than a cat's length away. I extend a limb and then two and, yes, I have it! I take hold of the tower's edge with my front legs. My back legs begin to slide on the slippery surface of the green plastic stone behind me. I've no choice but to surge ahead, lest I fall to the fiery pit of cold concrete below. I must leap forward, diminutive limbs or not. Faith of feline shall carry me to safety! I jump to the high tower with all of my might, but my back legs slip and I miss the mark. My front legs hold fast, my swords buried deep within the tower's edge. My hind legs claw and clamber my way up the vertical face to the summit. Success! I am a skilled climber and worthy victor of the competition. *Hear ye, hear ye, all ye can roam home as I am the winner of all things that anyone tries!* My, but the view is grand from up here. I see all, I know all, I am all. My Beautiful Tail cuts huge swaths through the air for all my queendom to witness. I sit now and take stock of what has become of my land.

I don't recognize my castle. What landscape is this? Tilting towers stacked to the heavens, battlements bundled and bandaged, crates and packages aplenty, superfluous, detritus strewn and infecting all of us. Battles were fought here, wars waged and won and lost and gone. It's darker now, colder. The furniture's been upended and blocking the windows, the very eye of summer's daylight dragon extinguished from the sky. What fleeting seasons come to pass, to end in winter's wintry wrath. How long was my slumber? A day? A decade? What potion did lace my last grand feast? Certainly wasn't fancy. A poison, at least!

But wait! What great skill I possesseth to easily ascendeth this very monolith! Indeed, this will be most advantageous in defending the castle. Perhaps the servants constructed these fortresses for my benefit! I've been too harsh and misjudged them. My Beautiful Tail swishes in disagreement. Ah, you're right, Beautiful Tail, if I weren't stern with the servants they wouldn't have a clue how to care for their queen and would surely perish. The human moron, in my estimation, is not to be overestimated.

O, what's this? My Beautiful Tail has found an obstacle on my tower's corner. Some sort of armament.

A tool. A token? 'Tis a round, thick thing, a hollowed brown ring. It could fit round the Simpleton's neck if one were wont to try. And not that I'm wont, but who wouldn't? *tap-tap.* It's a light oddity. *tap-tap.* This side of it is sticky! *tap-tap-tap.* What a funny sensation. I wonder what would happen if I sent it o'er the tower's edge? *tap-tap-tap.* And away it goes! O, a merry sound as it clunks against the concrete. Look how it rolls beneath the treasury for safe-keeping. I am successful yet again. Go ahead, Beautiful Tail, you may swish away now unencumbered.

A ward approaches. "Good day, dutiful ward." I nose the air with a slight trill. The human offers a high-pitched salutation and a hand approaches cautiously. There are a myriad of scents coming off the hand but mostly a spicy cinnamon. Poor thing is stressed. I'm sure they need a pet which always calms them down and has them smelling more agreeable. I allow their fingers to scratch beneath my chin and beside my ear. One, two… *Ok, that's enough.* Still I sense a cinnamon stench and pull my head away. Something's apaw here. I stare at the hand, daring it to try again. *Nothing gets past Your Queen,* my narrowed eyes infer. I mustn't be too congenial with the servants, you see, lest they forget who's in charge. The servant congratulates me on being a fair ruler and leaves me once again to rule on high. They appear to be looking for something. If it's common sense, that went down with the industrial revolution when they started making all that racket.

Human! What art thee doing? Get thee away from there! My eyes grow to the size of a dragon's in disbelief. They are huffing and puffing and pushing my treasured treasury! What treachery! They are pillaging my life's work! So many coins and wiry finds and shiny things. *They're all mine!* I'll miss many a nap depositing all of that back. O, it seems they require the sticky brown ring thing I just acquired and placed there. They're tearing strips from it and fastening them to my beloved boxes and packages! O, no, human, this won't do. How am I to access my corrugated castles if they're closed? "Servant! I say, servant! *Prrbbtt!?*" They're ignoring me whilst they continue their busy work. Dimwit!

What's this I hear? A skirmish. A strike? A knock! At the front gate! Tally ho, my troops! I shall gallop and greet the enemy. Make way! I leap ever so gracefully to the floor, *oof,* which was a little farther than calculated, my wee limbs slipping just ever so slightly beneath my ever so slight frame. I tear down the corridor, a foreboding blur, a sleek, black basilisk, to inspect and reject all visitors. But I see that the drawbridge is lowered! And without my consent! The border's been breached! I halt my sprint but because of the cursed concrete I slide ever so glamorously into a pile of overcoats. *Oof!* Fret not, dear reader, for Your Queen is fine and still the epitome of grace and grandeur, I assure you. Such is my narrative to which I am adhering steadfastly.

I free my head from amidst the coats to greet the foe that hast felled the gate. O, 'tis just one of my servants milling about. *Well, how on earth did you lower the drawbridge without my consent? Close it at once!* I widen my eyes and turn my left ear quickly. The ward saunters by passing loose fingers across my brow, and exits the castle, dutifully heeding my orders, however, to close the gate.

The dimension just beyond remains a mystery to me. On occasion I've set foot across the moat into the vast emptiness of space. Honestly, it was quite dreary indeed. Too many smells, too many sights, with not enough dens and too much daylight. No, I didn't like it a bit, no, not at all.

I saunter forth to guard the gate, a placement which also provides a good sightline down the hall to view the goings-on. Well, it did provide a good sightline until the servants sullied this place. Shame. What once was a clean, unfettered foyer to the castle is now a rampant wreck of ruin. A shambles. It is impossible to feel any sense of security. Felines are fickle, you see, and we shan't suffer fools, half-empty food bowls, or confusion. We must be sure of a thing before a thing is deemed safe and I am no longer sure of this slovenly place.

No, this is no place for a queen. It's no place for anything. O, what a tangled web they weave when the humans doth deceive their queen. I begin back down the corridor when I get a whiff of fresh hot chilli pepper. Panic.

I venture through the rubble of the foyer to the side room and the source of the scent. And there, sandwiched between a tower of green plastic stones and a pile of rectangular pieces that once hung on the wall lay a small container, enclosed except for thread bars criss-crossed all around. Through the threads I see a ghastly, blemished nose and eyes, diverted and hypnotized, staring at something, yet nothing. The Simpleton. One of its lazy eyes looks like it's trying to escape the cage. *Well, how did you get trapped in there, Simpleton?* My ears flutter the quick transmission. The Simpleton is silent. It stares blankly, solemnly. I approach the cell for closer examination. *Aye, ye silly sod, you've allowed yourself to get captured and I suppose you expect a pardon, yes?* I press my nose against the bars and inhale the pepper of panic. The

Simpleton's nose butts up ruthlessly against my own. "HISS! Such liberty to dare graze your queen!" I raise a swift paw and bat at the cage. "From hell's heart I stab at thee! I commit thee to the - *Prrbbtt!*" I trill unconsciously as I'm suddenly hoisted from the floor. What's this? A surprise attack! I must fight back! "I am QUEEEN!" I shriek. "Put me DEOOOWWWN!" The sky rumbles with my demands as I twist and coil but the giant's hands are powerful, inescapable. I am bandied about like a child's toy, flopped and jostled, this way and that. "Who dares handle me? Release me at once, barbarian!" The heathen hurls me carelessly into a tiny, dank dungeon. Before I can even raise a paw to strike I hear a *zzzip* as darkness envelops me. I turn round as best I can in my cramped quarters that I may gaze upon my ruthless aggressor. And I stare into their eyes with disbelief. The servant. MY servant! Deceived by the very hand I let pass my ear unscathed not minutes ago. O, but betrayal tastes bitter much like *the blood that you will surely shed upon my escape!* My eyes ablaze with fury, my ears flatten to the side as I ready to pounce on the perpetrator. The servant stands, only their foul feet within my sight, and I let out a loud, lingering growl. "You're lucky I'm in here slave, lest you lose an achilles with one swift swipe!"

Frightened, the slave retreats. I am left alone in the dungeon. But I am not undone. I paw my surroundings, an odd prison of tough cloth woven with a coarse thread and a mesh tapestry. The walls have some give yet seem impermeable to my swords. It smells faintly of pepper and catnip and vinegar. The scent triggers the visual of a White Giant with prodding hands and torturous interrogation devices. I now recall the last time I was quarantined in this confinement. I had forgotten the duplicity of the humans, the laughter as I was persecuted, crucified for being a complacent queen. 'Twas I who laughed last, licking the blood of the White Giant off my cunning claws.

I now know why the Simpleton was panicking. It would appear a mutiny is underway. The hateful humans have, for now, bested the best. I spy the Simpleton's cage. And, it appears, the worst.

Turns out I underestimated the traitors. I spy them now through the bars of my dungeon. They hurry to and fro, grunting, arguing, their hooves heavier than normal as they stomp past my prison. I hear the front gate open and close several times, the echoes of banging and clanging growing ever louder within the castle. More voices ringing, more clogs trampling through. The drums of war have reached a fever pitch and I can barely stand to watch the march. My boxes, my green stones, my crates, my bed, my bandaged packages, even my treasury. 'Tis a pillaging of my palace as thieves ransack and remove all my precious belongings. And the Dimwits were complicit. A river of commotion flowing by at a furious, turbulent pace, the ashes of ruin raining down as pirates storm the castle to plunder what remains. Alas, I am beaten, powerless. There are no stands left to make. Beneath me in my prison lies a servant's wrap, a tunic dyed green. They know this to be my favoured colour. An act of contrition? To cover the discretion? A veiled scheme to calm their queen? The attempt to acquiesce has only made me angry.

I peer into the ether before me, seeing the depth before feeling the fall. I fear there shall be no return, no redemption from what's to come. The descent into madness is not for the feint of heart, dear reader, and should ye close this tome, thy might be spared from horrors hence. But know this: mine is the queendom, and mine is the throne and mine is a vengeance the world's never known.

I turn to the back of my hovel to block out the horrendous happenings. It's all too much. The Simpleton remains silent. Dumbstruck, certainly, but that's status quo. I am alone to plot my escape and soothe my sorrow with fantasies of destruction and torment. No, no, I shan't go gently. What a whirlwind of terror I'll rain down on my tormentors! They should know who to blame for they've been warned: Hell hath no fury like a kitty cat scorned.

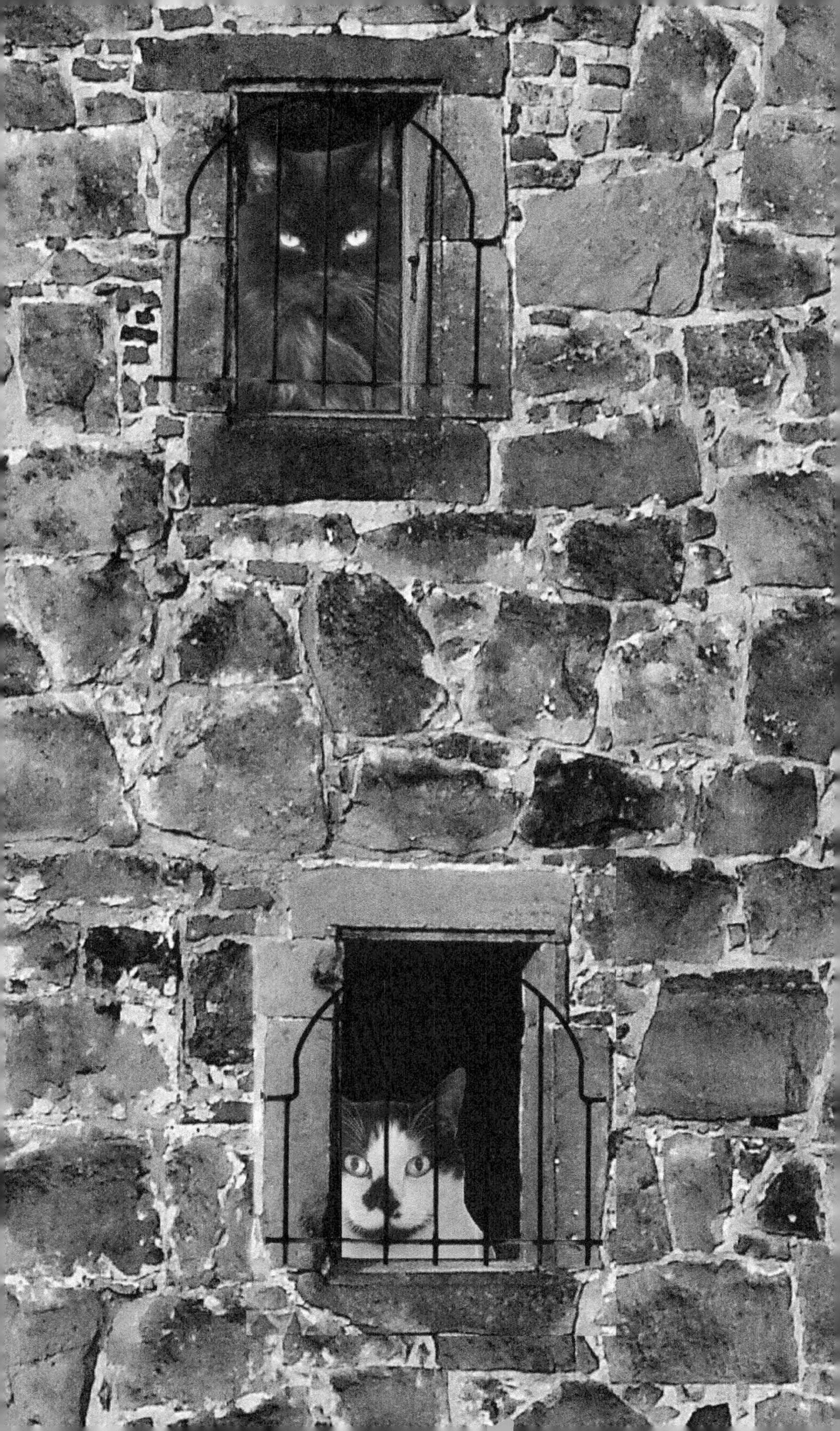

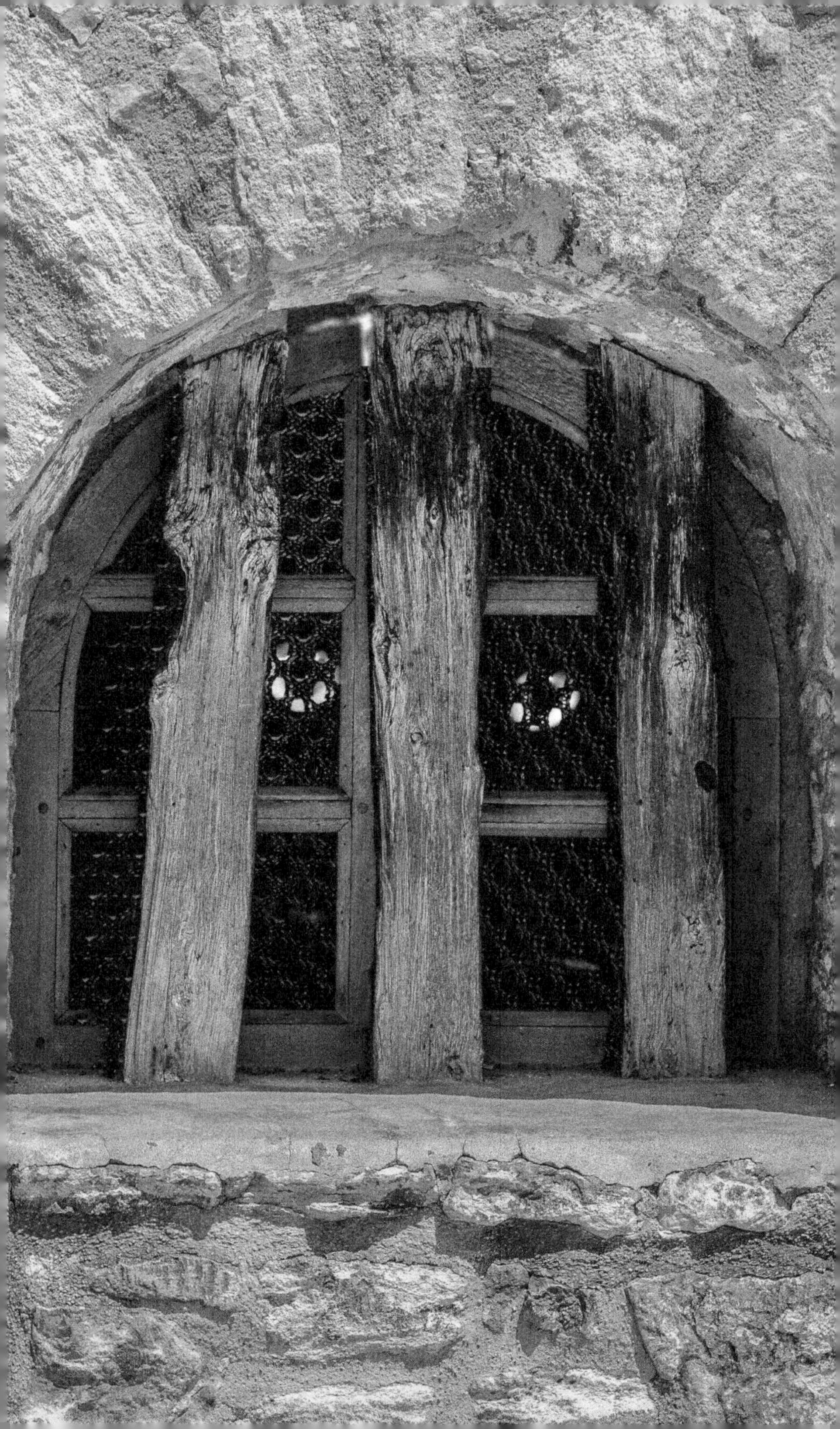

Chapter 4

There is nothing so confining as a competent prison made by idiots.

I should be able to escape. I am Queen Shorty Shoshobeans, after all. A force to be reckoned with in every realm. Creatures cower in fear nightly and daily at the mere mention of my moniker. These witless hominids are mere puppets in the machinations of my making. The only reason I allow them to stumble about this earthly terrain by my side is because of thumbs. Thumbs!

And yet, here I sit in squalor and solitude trapped in a Dimwit's device, my every attempt at escape a disappointment. Bewildering.

But I do believe I've discovered a weakness in my domain. The prison's hem is a woven cross-stitch, a tough twine that feels flimsy yet firm. From what I can discern, the bars of my cell are a mesh of mysterious material. I've tried slicing my way through but this drew too much attention from the traitorous servants who arrived quickly to thwart my getaway.

But at the top corner I spot a sliver of light seeping through, slightly larger than the mesh holes. I've pawed gently at the space and am certain I've expanded it. There is also a pleasing sound that results. *clink-clink.* I see something moving just beyond the space, a small thing bouncing up and down in response to my batting. *clink-clink.* What could it be? An insect? A flea? Too big to be a flea. A mouse? Too small to be a mouse, and my frame of reference informs me that all mice are pink and fuzzy with one misshapen black ear. 'Tis a foreign infiltrator, I suspect, one that warrants further study. *tap-tap-tap.* It responds with, *clink-clink-clink.* And so I *bat-bat-bat.* And again, *clink-clink-clink.*

Well, this is getting me nowhere. Is the thing alive? Is it a foe? If so, it doesn't go! The miniature mouse refuses to fear me and has lost my interest. But, wait. The sliver of light is no longer a sliver but has since grown to a full beam! A breach is shown where the light has shone! 'Tis not a foe at all, the curious flea, but a friend to a happy end! O, merry day, my escape is imminent.

I sit up tall on my haunches and gently reach through the opening with my front left paw. It fits! I extend my claws to grasp the exterior wall. Now what? Surely I can't fit through that small opening. Not that I'm portly, mind you. Generously proportioned, some might say. Rightly rotund?

For your edification, the excess flesh on my abdomen is actually an extra bit of skin round the belly whose purpose has confused humans for eons. Their theories range from protecting the abdomen during battle, ease of extension when running, or simply expanding to fill our gullet. None of this is true, however. No, it's just where we store extra hairballs for convenient and voluntary expression of displeasure. Like on that hideous rug, for example. You thought it a spontaneous act beyond our control? Heavens, no. How do you think we felines always have the time to make it to the unsightly carpet or to a servant's shoe before doing the deed? All planned.

Speaking of which, my current plan needs some work. My limb poking through the prison has squashed all but a freckle of light seeping through. O, but my luxurious fur surely takes up some of the space, half at least! I push my nose along my outstretched leg to the opening, my dainty legs stretching as far as they can to aid my height. I am powerful indeed as the passage opens further, wider. I hear a faint *zzzip*. My head is free! Now above the canopy, my eyes quickly scan my surroundings.

A desert. Barren. The towers and embankments and barricades and hideways now gone. No clear path of covert flight. Should that I escape, I can't flee to whence I came. The Simpleton's cell remains, its occupant still stupid. Voices in the distance. Booming footsteps echo. Voices getting nearer. Footsteps drawing closer. I've no time to route my liberation proper. A mad dash it must be to outskirts unknown. But any place is better than this. I must act now. I struggle to pull myself up with my left leg, still latched onto the outside of this contraption, but my hind legs aren't long enough to lurch me onward, my forward right leg clawing aimlessly within my cell. I jump and jump with no progress, my hope of egress fading. But I hear a clinking sound. Just to my left I see my little ally that aided my escape which was not a mouse nor a flea. 'Tis just a toy. A bauble, I think it. A jewel? A tiny little trinket! *Til we meet again, tiny friend. I bid thee farewell!* I transform into a cyclone of terror in my final push to freedom, my hind legs jumping and bouncing probably several centimetres at least, my Beautiful Tail thrashing madly to assist. It's happening! I'm escaping! I'm —

"My Queen!" A voice exclaims from above.

Damn! The insurgents are upon me. I've been found. Foiled! Perhaps I can pacify the person.

"Why, merry ho, good servant. Lovely day! *Prrbbtt?* Um, er, I wasn't doing anything, certainly not taking leave of this fine, um, domicile thou hast provideth for me. O, it's quite nice, especially the, um, south wing where I can really get some alone time, you know, some good, uh, meditation. There's nothing to see here. I see you're a bit wary of coming within striking distance, what with my histrionics from before. But listen. We're both reasonable, mostly, and perchance we could come to an understanding that is mutually beneficial. For instance, you let me go on my way and I won't slice you limb from limb. Deal? Watch it, human! Thy flesh shall melt at the fire of my blade. How dare thee touch the royal mane! *HISS!*" A hulking hand descends upon me, forcing my head back into my enclosure. But my front left paw won't move. The rebel somehow clamped it to the exterior at the place where it was previously stuck. I pull and I yank and hiss at my imprisoner as fumbling fingers feel for my fastened foot. "Leave me be, traitor! You're fiddling while Rome burns! I cast thee out!" I swipe with my right and stab its monstrous mitt and let forth a deafening roar. I'm thrown off balance and drop to the dungeon floor. The beam of light, once a beacon to freedom, shrinks to a sliver accompanied by the now familiar *zzzip* and then disappears altogether, punctuated with a conclusive *clink!* The foe do be the flea, ultimately.

Through my prison bars I spy the angry eye of the human, licking their wound. *Harsh words thee parried, sure, but just remember who striketh whom, servant.* The growl comes deep, from generations-past instinct, as trusting is the most unkindest cut of all. The human, my once faithful servant, departs down the hall leaving their once beloved queen to stew in solitary.

The banality of finality is fatiguing. If death should come, tell it I'm busy napping.

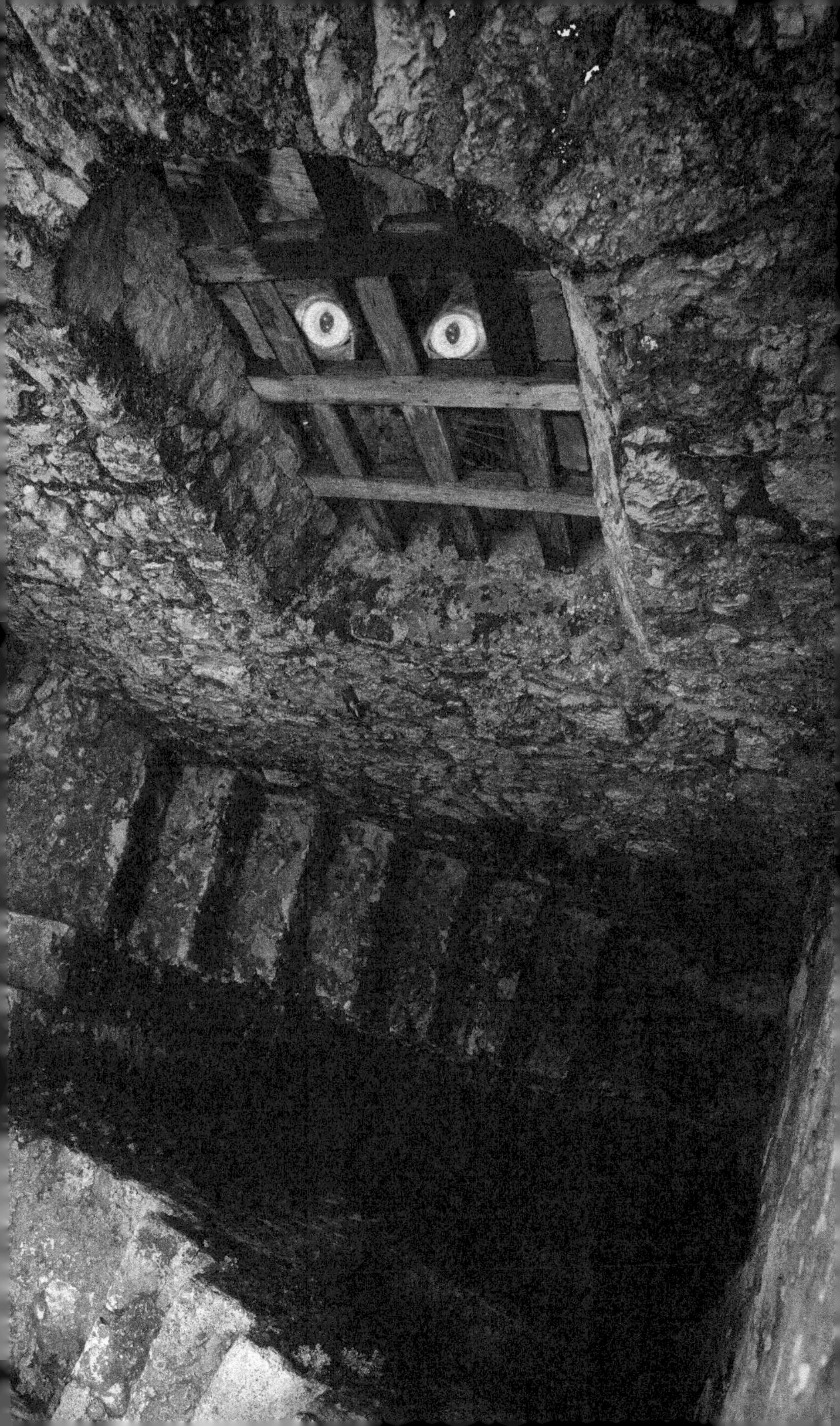

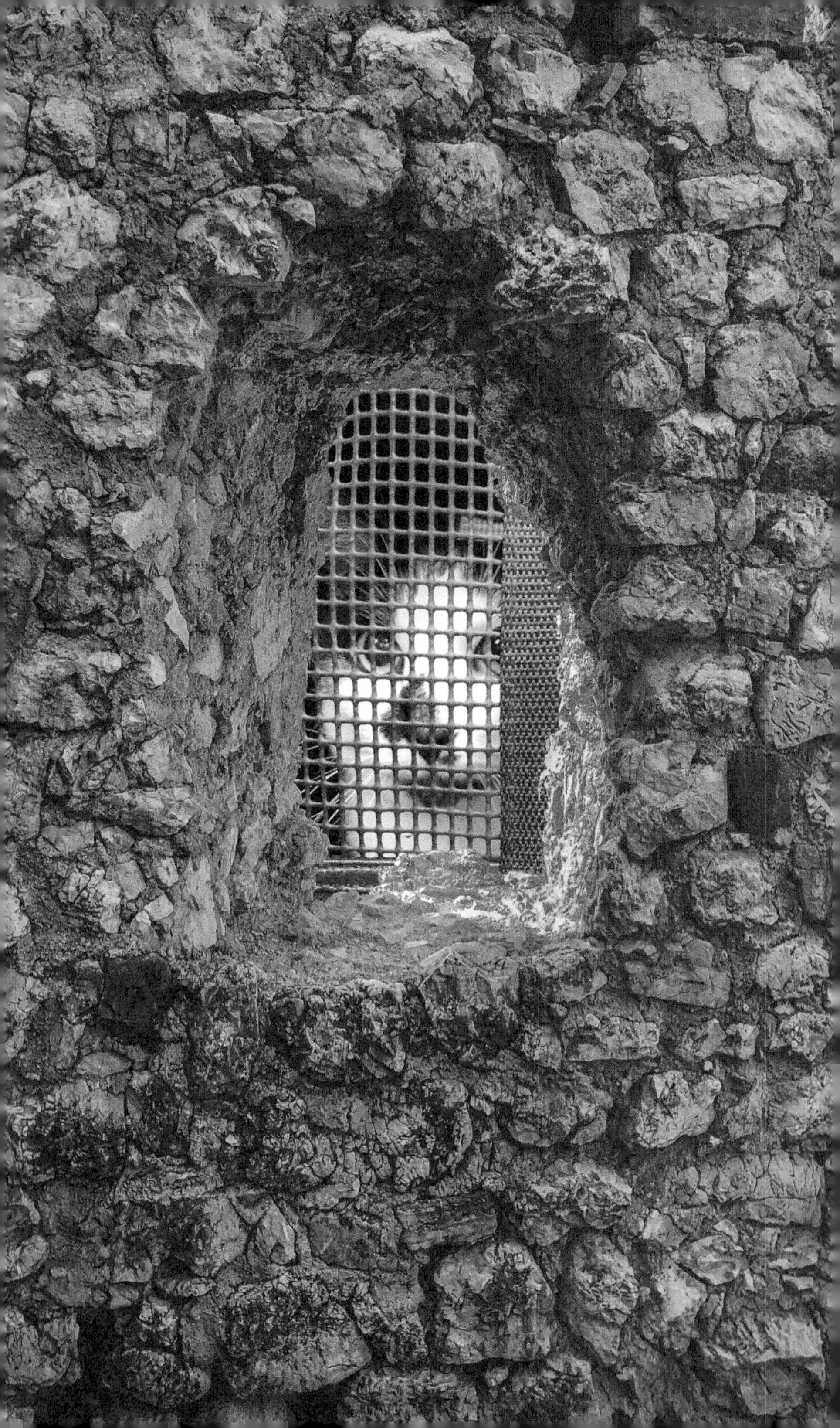

Chapter 5

Movement. An earthquake! A twister? Yes, I've flown aloft, my cell and all! Everything's a blur as I'm jostled side to side, hurled carelessly to and fro. The world outside turns and spins in a frenzied storm and I its harried hurricane eye. Perhaps I'll be fortuitous and land on someone wicked; the perpetrator who entrapped me, for instance.

I manage to turn round to get a better view through the mesh side of my confinement, my legs scrambling beneath me to find balance. I get caught up in the servant's lovely green tunic and suddenly feel all warm and fuzzy because of it. Curses! No, I am angry, enraged, quite affronted indeed! O, but the cloth does smell fine. But, O, how I am besmirched!

Wait! What's this? We're leaving the castle. I've not been beyond the moat since I can barely remember.

Not since... No, it can't be. We are destined for the White Giant! No, no, this is not good, not good at all. "Turn round this instant!" I cry out in a deafening rage. "Try as mine enemy might, I shall strike she and thee fast and fight to the last gasp!" My warning unheeded, we sally forth into open terrain.

    The elements fly by at too quick a pace. Fuzzy sights, foreign smells and sounds, flickering lights and yells from hounds. Overwhelmed may I be, dismayed I am not! I must stay vigilant, watching for any ambush, daggers at the ready, braced for the attack, comforted in the gorgeous soft green clothing and - curses!

    We're descending into a valley as strange fowl squawk and chirp and chime forebodingly. Peasants plod past. Metal elephants fly fast. The vastness of open space sprawls as we quicken. Warm glimmers of the dragon's eye flare through the prison bars to tease the upper hand as the war rages on. My how they do highlight the crimson colour in my glorious mane. Exquisite. O, that the commoners rushing by could catch a glance of my royal beauty now carried alongside them. What a gift for them to share mine air, to be in my presence, despite their ignorance, a queen amongst peasants. Yes, 'tis a philanthropic excursion this is, to boost their spirits! For mine is a queendom of benefaction, to help the downtrodden gaze upon me for just a moment of happiness to forget their dreary existence. *Thud.* My carriage and I and my daydreams brought crashing to earth.

"Human! Hast thou no comportment? O, that ye should sully thy queen in such a manner!" The ground reeks of refuse and wet canine and who knows what else, though nothing could be worse. *Blech.* The human has bent the knee and is peering one eye into my cage, just beyond a claw's reach unfortunately, and speaking in a tone most amiable, affable, but I'm certain deceitful. "You are captured, My Queen. While thou art still incredibly beautiful, your reign has ended." Or something to that effect, I'm sure.

"And yet I remain, disloyal drudge!" The ground trembles as I let out a drawn-out rumble. "You will pay for this treachery. And by the by, your lovely green tunic comforts me only a little!"

Oof. Hoisted aloft again, I'm hurled backward in my cell along with the green cloth which is now covering me completely. I shuffle it off just enough to free my face and now wear it as a cloak. Such indignity. O, but look how it shrouds everything but my eyes. A disguise! I am invisible. I see the world but the world sees me not. Commotions. A battalion of servant stumps stomping past. I hear a clicking noise, a clacking, a thwapping, human voices familiar and not, a lapping, a panting, a sniffing. A snout! Before, me, a lout, a slurping and burping dog sniffed me out! Despite my disguise it has detected me, its nasty nostrils pressing and flaring against my prison. "How dare thee, dog! Shoo, vile vermin!" I hiss and holler, and I attempt to smack its gnarly nose into oblivion but my swords catch the tunic and it goes over my head. I've been blindfolded! Servant and swine hath conspired against me! Covered again, my humiliation complete, I try to save face by letting out one more tumultuous roar but even that ends in a slobbering cackle, befuddled as I am.

I would take stock of my surroundings but am blinded by green. Small mercies. I take comfort in not seeing anyway. I hear the mutt's muted snortings and wheezings, more voices, and feel the jostling of motion once again. More shifting and stirring and locomoting. Another thud, a *zzzip* and *clink* and the human's high-pitched address. They uncover my royal cloak and the anonymity it hath provided. I deny them the satisfaction of my pleas but hurl daggers with my eyes nonetheless. *Unthread the rude eye of rebellion, seditious servant, or I'll unthread this lovely green tunic!* I dig my swords into the cloth so they stop messing it about. *It's mine, I tell you. MINE!* Dimwit.

Again my prison is shuttered and we set off crossing fields into the fray. I feel a rising as the servant heaves me higher but then my view is cut off; methinks the front of my cell is now held against the servant's chest, their arms enveloped around the prison. I could claw out their very heart if I had my druthers!

Alas, all my options lie scattered at my feet like shed claw sheaths and fur balls. But the lack of visual stimulation is somewhat calming, my surroundings somehow familiar. I take a deep breath, what feels like my first in a very long time, and sigh with a great deal of resignation and perhaps, even, the slightest bit of relief.

Nope, just resignation. If I am to battle the White Giant on this day, I shouldn't delay the next nap another minute. Instead of counting pink mice to lull into sleep, I'll count the misgivings of my servants. One thousand and one, one thousand and two, one thousand and...

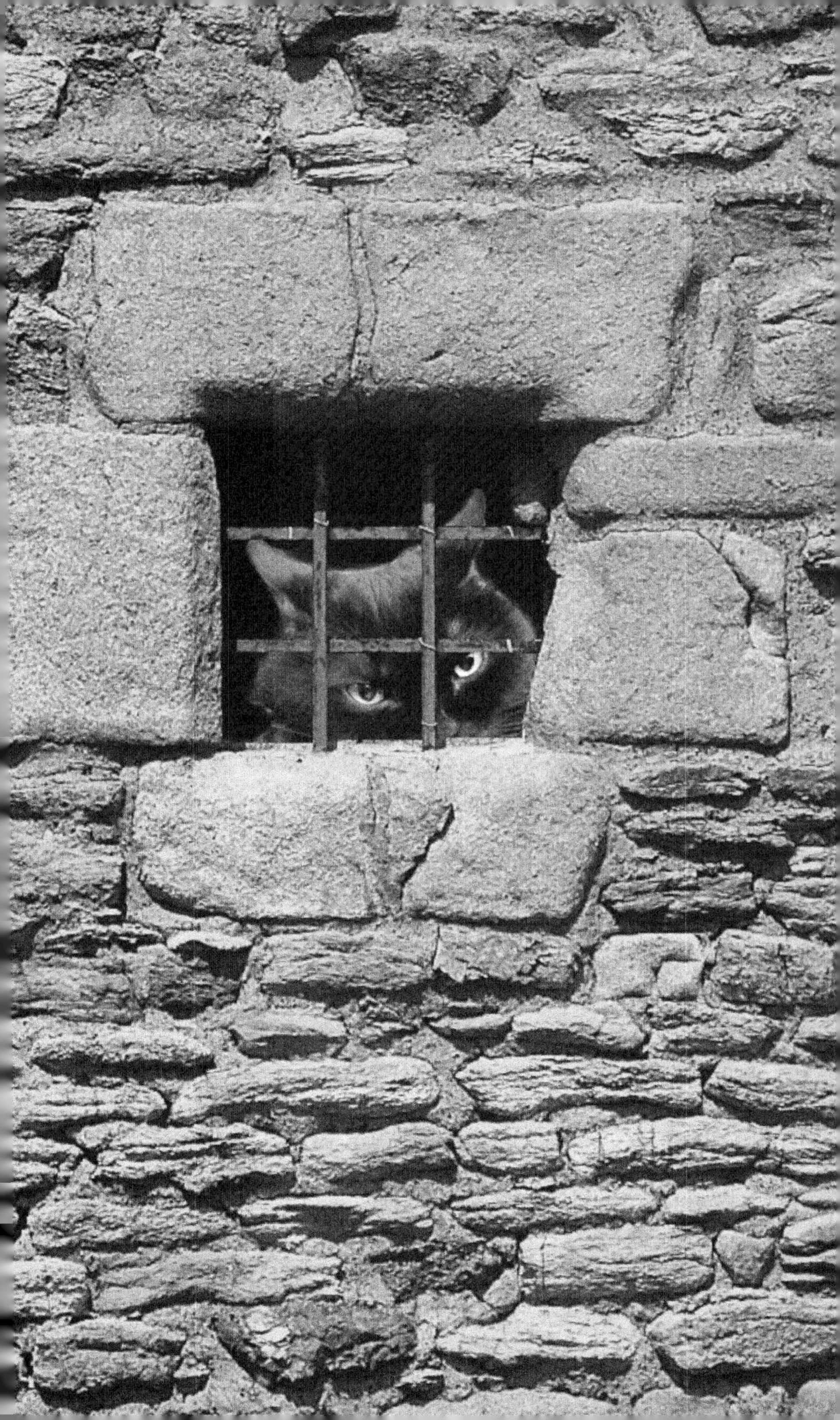

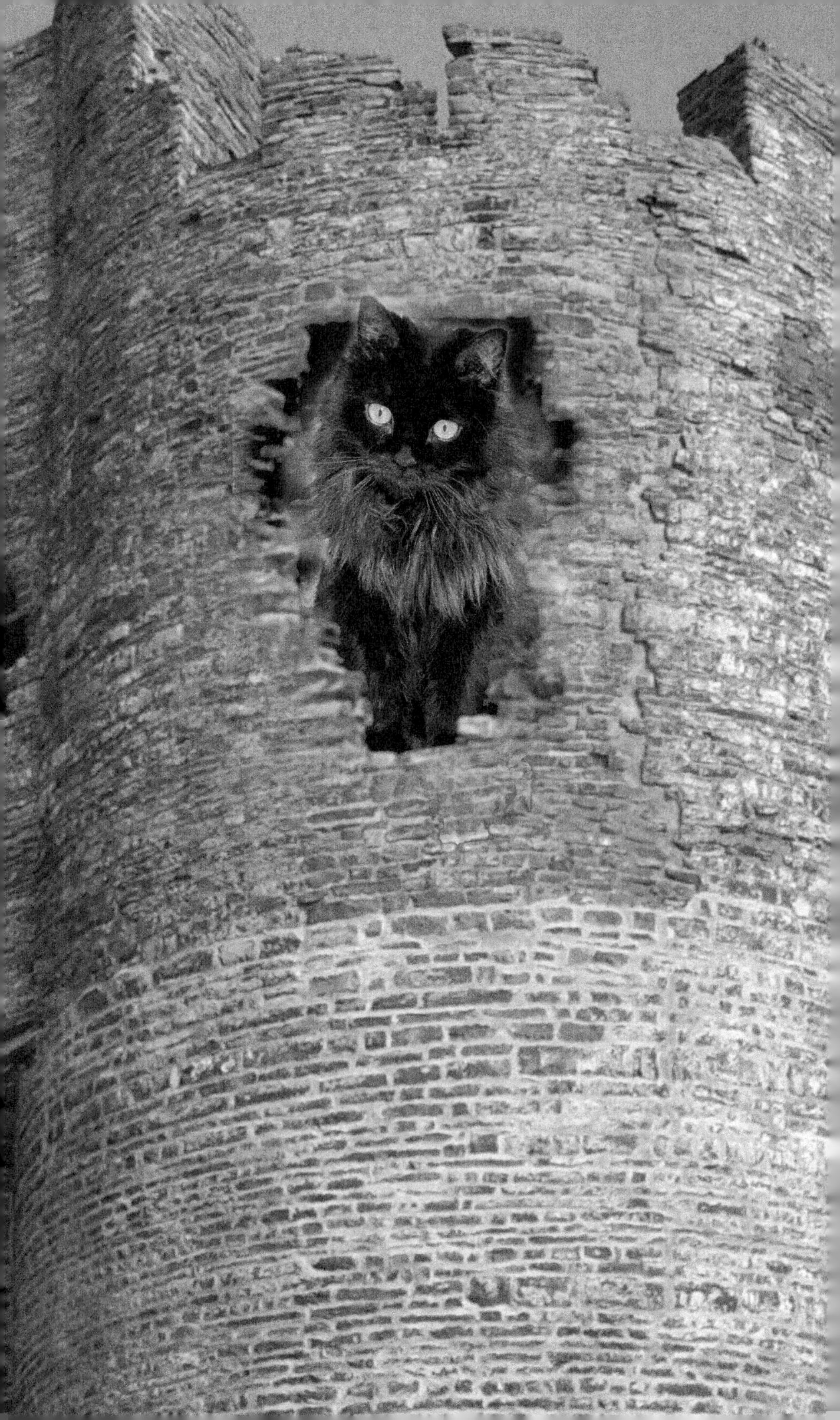

Chapter 6

A month has passed without nourishment. Perhaps a year. A fortnight surely. Honestly, the precise observance of time has never been an interest of mine; a queen never acknowledges its passage except when it pertains to feedings, nappies, and the malodorous moments passed after poopsies. Thus, I've chosen simply to ignore the concept altogether. But I am certain I've languished in solitary for at least forever.

Thud. My cell is dropped down discourteously. What's this I see before me through the mesh barrier? The Simpleton! It faces me from its own crude cell, much smaller than mine. Indeed my prison could hold twice as many, thrice! Aye, it surely befits a queen compared to the sullen Simpleton's confines. *'Tis a palace these fine woven walls compared to thy sorry surroundings!* I convey to the daft dolt through widened eyes. *Stop staring at me and flitting your ears, I don't know our destination either.* Surely its mother gave birth to her litter in a tree and this one fell from the tallest branch.

Bang! The earth just shook and went dark as if the universe had suddenly been snuffed out. What plague hast now befallen me? I've been pitched in a pit, buried alive, like some cast-off good-for-nothing runt of a litter. *Yes, I'm referring to you, Simpleton.* Even in pitch-darkness I see that one of its lazy eyes looks like it's about to take leave of its host. Can't blame it.

The dragon's eye sun, at least, has ceased its vexation, all outside commotions muffled. I'm in some sort of room. A tomb! Left to lie and die with no company but mine own. *Silence, Simpleton, I've been left to die alone in solitary, I don't need you simpering about!*

'Tis under the shield of darkness when I am truly powerful, omniscient. The blackness of dark matches my coat and I become the shadow, the cunning, the strike you don't know is coming. My eyes pierce the hollow to hunt for an egress, the servants nowhere near to thwart my escape attempt this time.

Through the cross-stitch windows I can see my enclosure appears entirely blocked. I paw again at my surroundings. To the side, the sturdy textile wall is malleable but as yet impassable. I paw again and again and again, scraping my swords against the strange material. I can't give up. I won't! *scrape-scratch-scritch-scratch.* Hm. There is no change. Or perhaps there is. *scratch-scritch-scrape-scratch.* Quite a pleasing sound, really. Let's try with the other paw, my right, which isn't as deft as my left, but let's give it a go. *scrape-scrap-scritch-scratch.* It's proving quite hypnotic, rhythmic, sonic. *scrape-scratch-scrap-scritch.* As my muscles move, my mind stills, my focus hones. The repetition is calming, familiar. I forget now where I am, even what I am doing. I am scraping this strange textured wall for some reason in sundry contemplation again and again and nothing is changing, yet still I persist. But everything is changing. I am not trapped simply because another tells me it's so, for my mind flows freely into and through and out these walls. Indeed, I've never felt so free here in my protected sanctum. *scratch-scrape-scritch-scrape.* That enlightenment should arrive in a shroud dark as my mine delights me not a little. *Mark me, Simpleton! Witness the grandeur of my ascension! scrape-scrap-scritch-scratch.*

If I weren't so busy being enlightened, I might have noticed a *click.* And a *creak.* And the blasted beam of the dragon's eye daylight shining down upon me. But

I am lost in my meditation. *scratch-scrape-scrawl-score*. Score! I've made a mark! Produced a puncture! Alas, my sword is stuck! I pull and yank at the textile wall, now seemingly made of stone, and I'm suddenly keen to the sunlight and the shrill yapping of my subversive servant's voice. They speak in a pleasant pitch but I'm certain it's only to bewitch! "Oh, My Queen, trying to escape the boot of the carriage are you? Pointless!" And suddenly I am ascending alright, just not in the transcendental sense. My cell and I have again been lifted up, jogging me side to side which freed my sword from the stone. Excalibur hast not a thing on this queen.

The view from my prison passes fast but I'm sure I just caught a glimpse of more hellhounds near by, their offensive snouts sniffing me out to bring about my demise. Come closer, ogres, and I shall slice thy snouts and throats! Another *thud*, a *slam*, a *chug*. I believe my chamber and I have been placed on the servant's lap, the warmth familiar even through the coarse fabric beneath. A container has been placed facing mine. *O, Simpleton, thou art here again! I keep forgetting on purpose that ye exist.* It stares at me blankly, brainless. It's been shocked into suspended animation! Poor, stunted pest can neither plead nor grunt protest. I would tell it not to worry if I thought it capable of basic comprehension. And by the stench of its breath the only thing it's been comprehending is its own bottom. *You're disgusting, is what I'm saying, Simpleton, just really, really rank.*

The ground below me begins to tremble and grumble. My cage shifts rhythmically back and forth, side to side. Bumps. Thumps. Jolts. I extend my swords through the lovely green tunic into the prison hem for support. I spy the rebels to my side facing away from me. My brow furrows and my ears slant back as I let forth a grumble of my own. "I say, slave, I find the manner of my transport most disagreeable." They ignore my protestations and persist in the turbulence of the carriage. I look to the Simpleton for a hint of assistance, a sign of situational awareness, a single note of intelligence, and find not a one.

I must admit the Simpleton is my greatest failure as queen. It arrived to my queendom a child, a boy, a forlorn, fussy little shrimp of a thing, with boldness and flair and not a brain cell to spare. He stood up to the servants which amused me, and stood up to me which intrigued me. The nerve it would take to challenge all within the castle, a pint-sized speck no bigger than the tip of my Beautiful Tail, I thought him destined to be a knight or a ninny, and I wagered hopeful on the former. O, but I was optimistic back then.

At first, he was so brash he was boorish, climbing the servant's legs like trees, going potty in the planters, clawing the furniture like a feral beast, and I disciplined him upon every misconduct. After a week of corrective action, he fell in line and I accepted him as my apprentice; the fact that I needed to expand my army to adequately defend the castle certainly had much to do with my decision.

Though he was initially disobedient, the one trait that was immediately redeemable was his watchful eye, lazy as it was. Because it certainly wasn't his appearance. My heavens, he was unpleasant to look at. Ears too big, eyes wide-set, and he looked permanently filthy, like an albino rabbit that stumbled into a puddle of black ink. He followed me everywhere, did everything I did, ate where I ate, scratched where I scratched, slept where I slept. He even proved a fair sword-fighter and himself a nimble competitor in our military drills, sprinting the lengths of the castle's corridors back and forth and back again. We laid out surprise attacks on each other several times a day keeping our skills and our minds sharp. Though he never quite understood the point of my morning and evening rounds - checking the entire castle for intruders, weaknesses, shadows, and sprites - he nonetheless proved an earnest pupil and, dare I say it, a trusted comrade.

But, over time, he insisted on doing the one thing I did not give him permission to do. He grew. Tall. Big. His legs soon became so long he could jump to the counters and climb ladders with ease. The dirty rascal would climb to all of the castle's lookouts and act like a king. I swear he'd be laughing at me from his new heights, my petite frame preventing me from following suit. And he soon took advantage of his stature. If I were hunting the pink fuzzy mice, he would get overly excited and leapfrog over me and bound off the walls and take the prize for himself. There was no thrill of the kill to be had for the queen! Even whilst I slept, he would rouse me with a surprise attack, not understanding there was a time and place for such things. It became ever so tiring fighting off a lanky lout who couldn't control his increasing strength. But all of it I could forgive, every transgression I could forget, if he had just stopped being so damned dependent.

For example, if I was getting pet-pets from the servants, he would get so jealous he'd leap up and challenge me for a place on their lap. Wherever the servant would go, the Simpleton would follow. No longer was he loyal to the queen, he soon favoured the slaves! The second they would leave the castle he would start wailing away as if abandoned by his mother. Upon their return, he would whine endlessly asking why he was abandoned. It was embarrassing, really. He stopped standing up to them, and never did he ever commit even the most comical misconduct against the humans, so concerned he was with being, ugh, good.

Some soldier he turned out to be. If there's one thing I absolutely won't tolerate, aside from dirty litter boxes, more than two belly rubs, the repugnant rug, shadow demons, small sprites perched halfway up walls masking as spots, half-empty food bowls, strangers, cages, rotten apples, long legs, loud noises, mornings, filthy floors, and servants who don't know their place and become traitorous saboteurs, it's simpletons.

Thus, through a lot of aggravation, my once-trusted apprentice became little more than a nuisance to me and I soon regarded him - it - as nothing more than a lowly jester in my court, a tiring trifle I could pawn off on the Dimwits to amuse them so I could nap. A promising comrade-in-arms ended up a displeasing gad with no charms. And now, with the ground beneath us trembling, heading to parts unknown and a fate uncertain, it stares at me from behind its bars in absolute panic. The helpless Simpleton could have been so much more if it stayed in line under my capable paw. Surely death would come swift if forced to fend for itself. Now I look upon the dunce with such disappointment, a lot of loathing, and yet an inkling of envy. Having nothing, nothing can it lose. I flick my right ear sideways and back, leering at the traitor. *You're lucky, Simpleton, for thy lack of wit permits the ignorance of danger.* Its one good eye tracks generally in my direction. *What I'm saying is that you're stupid.*

I was unprepared for the sudden lurch and I'm thrown to my side mid-leer. "My Queen," a slave addresses. "We hath arrived at the destination of your doom. Prepare for the fury." Movement. My cell and I are being transported again, *and with very little care, mind you!* I'm tossed tumultuously about whilst they avoid addressing my displeasure. Dimwits.

Onto the battlefield once more. Humans and their clumsy stumps, the scent of stale and fresh dog urine all around, chirps and beeps and bells and honks fill the putrid air, my prison paraded through the streets of town. My Beautiful Tail strains to swish as she is again caught beneath the green tunic. 'Tis an inglorious end to my reign, this march, but at least I look good in green.

We seem to be crossing a series of drawbridges and glass gates and enter what I assume to be the torture chamber of my undoing. The White Giant, with their cold instruments and prodding fingers, will be no match for the wrath I will wreak upon my release!

But something seems awry. There is always a scent dissonance within the White Giant's quarters, an uncomfortable juxtaposition of fear, recently disinfected floors trying to mask excrement and wet-dog, and a plethora of treat-treats. Absent even are the loathsome odours of the sanctimonious White Giants themselves. No, this is a different station of suffering entirely. The floor is adorned with patchwork rug that smells artificial but is not altogether repulsive. Somehow I believe it to resemble the coat of a leopard though I've never seen one in the wild. Well, I've never been in the wild, so what would I know? But for the intrinsic intelligence passed down through my royal bloodline, some observations and wisdoms procured along the way, I've no specific knowledge of my feline cousins. But I do know they must hunt for themselves and they don't get treat-treats whenever they desire them. How uncivilized.

A silver gate slides opens and we enter a small room that smells of wood and metal and corrugated cardboard and slave sweat. The servant speaks to me in a rising intonation that doesn't imply impending doom at all but I'm not so easily swayed. The gate opens again and I am escorted down a long corridor with the same rug I saw and smelled before, a scent that could only be improved with my assuming ownership here and there and everywhere.

I've been placed on the floor, gently this time. *O, what magnanimity ye can finally afford, slaves,* I call out in a huff. That I might forgive such transgressions past through meagre niceties. *Methinks not!* There appears to be a solid gate before me. Nay, a drawbridge.

A *click*. A *chunk*. The drawbridge is opened. I am carried in and, again, set down lightly on the floor, its surface a bleached wood that is not at all like the cold, foul-smelling ground I was expecting. If the White Giant changed quarters since the last torturing this is at least an upgrade.

The Simpleton is next to me, surely having quite the fit having lasted this long without its beloved servant fawning over it like a feeble baby. But what's this? The servant bends the knee and addresses the Simpleton like, well, a feeble baby! They call out to it in their favoured term of gibberish, "hoozagooboi," which makes no sense to me. I imagine it translates to imbecile. I hear a *click* and a *clink* and a *creak* and watch as the Simpleton escapes its enclave, none the worse for wear. But, honestly, who could tell with that mottled mug. The servant picks it up and leads it away and I am thankful. At least I can lie alone with my thoughts, peaceful that the journey has, for the time being, paused. Perhaps the White Giant has already begun the experiments. Or perhaps the Simpleton is free! I hear it wailing away now, the Dimwits speaking in their piercing pitches. Why doth I remain entrapped whilst morons run amok? They've all conspired against me. The jester, it seems, plans to have the last laugh whilst I meet my doom trapped in this dungeon. But I shan't. I won't! I am still queen, after all. I shall rule with an iron paw for as long as I can! Or at least until my next nap, which hopefully isn't far off.

A servant kneels down next to my cage and addresses me softly. "My Queen, thou art more beautiful than ever!" *zzzip*.

I see a space reveal itself at the front of my cell just as I am willing it open. Yes! My gaze is powerful indeed as the breach gets bigger and bigger. Glory day, I have managed to unravel the tapestry of my prison! Now is my chance to escape. I peek my head out to gauge safe passage. The White Giant is nowhere in sight. Perhaps they hide behind my prison to pounce! I step one cautious paw beyond my cage and careen my neck around to check for attackers. No one. One more step, and another, and another, and I've escaped my enclosure entirely! Freedom feels fine indeed, as does the wood floor which feels soft and warm on my feetsies. But I mustn't let my guard down for the White Giant and their army could strike at any moment. I look to the left and to the right. It appears I am in a vestibule off a corridor, not dissimilar to my castle in fact. I continue forth staying low, creeping surreptitiously, so covert that none can see that I've freed myself from the dungeon. The servants continue their shrill speech, acting as if everything is normal, but they are dullards and can't see me as I glide so close to the floor, stealthy as a ninja.

I come upon a small room, a closet. What's this? A poopsies depository. *My* poopsies depository! Smells just like home. What manner of puzzlement is this predicament? Where is the White Giant? Where is the onslaught? Where is the army of my destruction? I sidle around the corner, careful not to suffer a sneak offensive by unknown interlopers. I enter a small room to my right filled with green plastic stones and boxes and barricades stacked to the ceiling. Familiar sight, similar fragrance, but I am not mistaking the difference. I make a note of the opportune hiding spots between and behind towers and blockades. I advance down the corridor. For some reason the servants keep following my path which is odd since I am not visible when camouflaged as a ninja. I hear the Simpleton mewing plaintively for attention whilst the humans continue to call out to their invisible queen. All the while, hints of recognition of castles past waft by. More hollow stones, cardboard boxes, and a rug. My rug? Yes, 'tis my detestable rug! I sniff it disbelievingly. Even now I can smell the vomit of displeasure I will express upon it in due course. And there's my couch, my chair, my glass table I lie on when I need a servant's attention, and my side table that must be cleared of all objects all of the time, especially when I need a servant's attention. 'Tis the remnants of my castle strewn about this new place! Aye, the servants rescued all of my possessions after the previous onslaught! A curious benefaction considering they hath waged mutiny.

"Queen! My Queen!" a servant hollers, bending the knee at my feet. I freeze, turning my ears sideways, slowly gazing upwards in the direction of the human voice. *Thee sees me? How could this be? But I slither secretly as a snake! Art thou a wizard?* I approach their outstretched fingers cautiously and take several shallow sniffs. Boxes, plastic bags, this servant is currently content and feeling pleasant. Perhaps they've gone mad. I scan my surroundings quickly and glare back at them. *Where hast thou taken me? Where is thine army? Aye, ye play such fantastic tricks but I am no fool. On guard!* I spring-load my body, leaning on my back legs, ready to pounce on any incoming peril. I am certain that trouble is apaw. Or perhaps trouble really is a foot? Yes, I should strike the human's foot. But it's not within striking distance. Well I have to strike something! Where's the Simpleton when you need it?

"Queen, My Magnanimous Queen, we are eternally regretful for the attempt at your throne and beg forgiveness for our crimes and all the injustices you've suffered ever."

They reach a pasty palm out to touch my crown but I back away and raise a parrying paw. *What's this? You request that I forget your evil? Never! Bring your hand within striking distance, I dare you!* I narrow my eyes to punctuate the warning. Definitely frightened and undoubtedly remorseful, the servant retreats with their head hung in shame. *That's right, shameful treasonist. You imprisoned me for an eternity and I shan't forgive so easily. Walk away in shame. Shame!*

I stand statuesque until the servant falls back to a more appropriate breadth. When their back turns I take refuge behind a nearby tower to monitor the humans, still uncertain of the their objectives, and become invisible while keeping one eye trained on them. I am only visible to the servants if they can see both mine eyes. I'm not sure why, it's just how it works.

I can see the mouth-breathers have retired to the couch and are dining on something that smells disgusting, though the box it arrived in looks enticing. They're eating, talking, laughing, looking around the castle, pointing, plotting, perhaps conspiring. After I freed myself from prison, they haven't seemed intent on throwing me back or reprimanding me. Must be some ploy to gain my trust. I feel my brow furrow, my ears turning back against the human chatter. I glare at them with one squinted eye as they now move about the castle surely up to no good and I vow to rage, rage against their insurrection for I shall not go gentle into that good -

"Your Royal Meowjesty, would you like some *foooood?*"

My eyes widen and my ears turn forward. Food? Provisions? A proffer? Could it be the humans have no desire to usurp their beloved ruler? Could I have been wrong? Is being wrong a thing that is possible? No, that's not it, can't be, I've never been wrong about a thing that has ever transpired. My Beautiful Tail cuts huge low arcs through the air and against the lovely wooden floor so much preferred to my prior castle's ghastly stone. Aye, but the path is smooth that leads on to danger. But now the usurpers are offering me supper. I glance over my precious belongings in this strange place, this new castle, my... home? Ah, yes. Indeed, I had oft mentioned to the servants of my distaste for the concrete floor and the uncleanliness of my residence. I look back at the human who is still waiting for my response. Instead, I am the one asking questions.

"*Prrbbtt?* Is this my new palace? Have thee extended an olive branch to beg forgiveness?"

"Aye, Your Royal Meowjesty. Thou hast successfully procured through royal demand the acquisition of a finer castle and henceforth we seek only to serve thee until queendom come. Now, how about that *fooood?*" As I expected and knew all along and never once questioned, I am victorious! Also, famished.

Oh heavens, yes, the foooood of which you speaketh doth sound pleasing. I saunter over with my Beautiful Tail tall and curved in communication. "Prepared a kill for me, hast thee, ward?" I trill.

"Queen Shoshobeans, might that I appease My Queen with a bounty of mice entrails and duck confit?"

"I say, that will do nicely," I trill again and nose the air. The dutiful, repentant slave has acknowledged the error of their ways and is preparing my feast on the counter. A *crack*, a *creeeaaak*, a *slurp*, and the *clinking* of metal on glass as they skin and bone and braise the prey. They set my meal before me on the floor. I sally up to sniff the kill, but pause to acknowledge a lingering unsettling feeling. I peer up at the remorseful rebel, my Beautiful Tail swishing this way and that does all the talking. *I am pleased with the provisions but not at all with you. Get thee away!*

The servant retreats to let their queen be but I turn to watch them as they flee to ensure no infringement on my dining. But, what's this? The Simpleton sidled up to my bowl when I wasn't watching! It is helping itself to my meal, the servants having provided just one dish this eve. Perhaps supplies are scant, or there are few beasts roaming this part of the land that we must ration our fare. I walk up beside the Simpleton and place my head on top of its vacant skull and apply pressure, my front leg wrapping round its scrawny back. *O, no, Simpleton, this won't do at all. You know the rules. The queen eats first and the jester has what is left. Go jest somewhere else until I'm finished.* The Simpleton obeys and slinks away. Miraculously, it has shut up but keeps lurking around as if it lost its soother, continually looking to the servants for allowance to explore the new surroundings. *You are a disappointment and a disgrace to the queendom, you hideous Holstein cow!* It ignores my umbrage, or doesn't understand. Most likely the latter. At peace, I can finally enjoy the hunt of the day. Unquiet meals make ill digestions causing expressions of displeasure on couches and cushions.

The bowl now completely empty save for half its contents, I retreat to a dark corner to lick my chops and survey the schema of my new home. Actually, no, I am not surveying anything at all. I am tired. My eyelids grow heavy. Darkness has fallen, but I am in no mood or manner for the Night Watch. Out the corner of my eye I spy a rodent loudly lapping up my leftovers. I wonder where a queen could rest in this palace of pests?

I recognize the distinct sound of crinkling plastic from a chamber down the corridor. I shake off the sleepiness and proceed cautiously to the room where the servants appear to be assembling my bed. *Good work, servants*, my Beautiful Tail announces with a curvaceous whip of the tip as I meander to the middle of the space to take a seat for proper supervision, anticipating a lengthy nap. I lick my paw to wash my face and am interrupted by a servant's voice which is louder than usual. "My Queen, thou art more beautiful than all the queens in all the lands!" Methinks they are trying on their threatening tone, but that doesn't accord with their praise.

My Beautiful Tail a whip, my paw raised mid-wash, I admonish the servant with a glare. *Thilenthe, thervant, thy voithe vextheth me!* What's this? Why do I sound like this? Something is awry. My eyes wide, I search my surroundings for an answer. The servants are laughing. I knew it! 'Tis not my new castle, 'tis a colosseum of persecution, and this bed frame a gladiatorial contest! My hackles up, my tail awry, my tongue… cold. I look at the servants, still giggling maniacally. *Thervant? Why ith my tongue cold? It theemth ath if I can't thpeak properly.* I look at my paw still in mid-air, catch the mild scent of the hunt consumed, lick twice more and stand stoically staring at the servants. *I say, servant, what was I saying? Were you laughing? What is happening? O, yes, my bed, please carry on.*"

"Queen Shoshobeans, you have a Beautiful Tail! SO BEAUTIFUL!"

I frown at the shouting. *Slave, I am aware, now cut your tone by half or I'll halve your tongue.* Indeed, the origin of the phrase, "cat got your tongue" is because we simply refuse to tolerate yelling, and humans are excessively cacophonous the majority of their waking hours. But the ancestors soon learned that trying to shred at the human's head didn't exactly work in our favour, so we have since learned to quell our killing instinct. Rest assured, it's still there, whenever we need it.

The slave knows well not to approach their queen but responds insolently by hurling a tomato at me. Such defiance! O, what's this? It's not a tomato, it's some sort of vermin, a roundish rodent, a white weasel of a thing. I paw at it and it makes a glorious scratching sound along the wooden floor. Look at how it seeks to escape by rolling away. I pursue the pest, batting it and swatting it and chasing it out of the sleeping quarters and down the corridor. *You can't escape or defy the queen! No one can!* I bound about as it continues to scurry away. I take one large, lobbed leap and end up head-butting it and me into the floor. I shake off the stars and funnel the tiny beast under my body and sit on it. Queen Shorty Shoshobeans, the Vanquisher! I fall to the side, holding the creature in my claws as my hind legs beat it into submission. I check my quest. Success! It moves not! What's this? Movement. Out the corner of my eye. The Simpleton! It's upon me, wanting to plunder my prey. *Have at it, Simpleton, I've already bested the pest.*

I see a servant exiting the sleeping quarters and heading for my front room. Seems they want to race! I run down the corridor, slip between the servant's stumps, maneuver through the towers, jump to my couch, and then vault to the top of a barricade where the human is heading. *What hast thou planned for these battlements. Speak, slave!* My eyes wild, my Beautiful Tail in charge. "What the frrrllll?" I trill reflexively as the servant's gaudy hands take hold of my delicate frame and toss me to the floor.

I lick their sordid scent off my fine coat and glare at the human who has taken one of my green plastic stones to the sleeping quarters. What insolence! The other servant is walking to the cooking gallery so I hurry to walk in front of them and then slow down because they're walking too fast to pay attention to my distaste for disloyalty. What's this? The servant stomps right past, swiping at my Beautiful Tail! It's all right, my Beautiful Tail. I wash my Beautiful Tail of the filthiness left behind. I lick and clean and wash and preen. Aye, 'tis good to feel clean. 'Tis good to feel this floor of wooden planks, though it could smell a lot better. I roll onto my back twist and turn and stretch my legs long, extending my claws and relishing in the reach. A servant comes upon me and I curl my front paws in and gaze up at them with my belly exposed.

"O, my Queen, thou art the cutest and sweetest and most precious of all the earth's creatures." I turn my head up and curve my body like the letter C. *I know.* I let their now fragrant fingers tousle the fur under my chin and behind my ears. I wonder if they will try for the belly? Their hand pulls away and brushes against my front paws. Yes, yes, I think they will. Their hand ventures lower to my white undercoat. *Tee hee!* The first one tickles. O, joy! The second one prickles. I stare at them, wide-eyed, Beautiful Tail a flurry. *Come on, servant, I dare you.* And a third! Yes! I take hold of their hand with all paws and careful claws, grabbing their fingers to chomp down ever so lightly. Dutiful wards they are, I must remind them who's in charge, you see. I grant leniency upon their protestation and release them. I roll onto my front and sit up to survey my new home.

It must be middle of the night by now. The servants are dousing the lanterns one by one. The Simpleton watches my every move from atop a tower of green stones. My couch is in place, my carpeted throne awaits, my chair is prepared for me, my rug is ready for my expressions of displeasure. My new palace seems quieter than the last, less echoes traveling down the hall, less shiny elephants rumbling by outside. I inhale deeply which yields a yawn. All lights are out now and the servants have retired to their sleeping quarters. I venture down the castle corridor for a last inspection and to attend to some last-minute doodie duty.

Ah, my poopsies depository. I am grateful it survived the battle, though I admit I would not have been opposed to soiling this entire castle if 'twere not up to snuff. I would have also enjoyed seeing the servants argue about the reason, wondering what "message" I was sending. The directive they have failed to decode is this: What idiot would place a depository where I don't like it? Dimwits.

But on with the business at hand, and then a follow-up scratch upon the plastic dome. *scratch-scritch-scrape-scratch.* The business, unfortunately, is not being buried as my instincts suggest it should. Indeed, my only quarrel with the plastic dome is that it does a poor job in covering my poopsies. *scrape-scratch-scritch-scratch.* Hm. *sniff-sniff.* There is no change. *scrape-scrap-scritch-scratch.* Hm. *sniff-sniff.* Or perhaps there is. My instincts whisper to me that this scratching motion will remove my waste from my sight, but scratching the plastic dome does little more than amuse me which is honestly good enough for me. 'Tis a pleasing sound, my nails on this scratchy surface. O, joyous sounds, quite musical really! The repetition is calming, familiar, like I've done this before but I can't recall when specifically. I go faster and faster. *scrape-scratch-scrap-scritch-scrape-scrap-*

"QUEEN!" a servant bellows from the sleeping quarters. "WHAT BEAUTIFUL MUSIC THOU HAST BESTOWED UPON US! THANK YOU, YOUR HIGHNESS!" Ah, my admiring servants. They are always appreciative of my talents, and I am nothing if not a charitable queen.

I make my way through the castle once more, avoiding and cursing the mess the servants have made. Stones and boxes and barricades, towers and armaments and fortresses misplaced. If I weren't exhausted from missing my catnaps today I might take it upon myself to do some more investigating. But alas, my head, even heavier from the crown on this day, needs to rest. I spy the Simpleton nestled beneath the couch, half-sleeping and keeping a lazy eye locked on my every move. I take leave and venture into the sleeping quarters and tuck just inside the now finished bed frame beneath the cover of night. *O'er the hem and 'neath the bed, I slink to rest my weary head...*

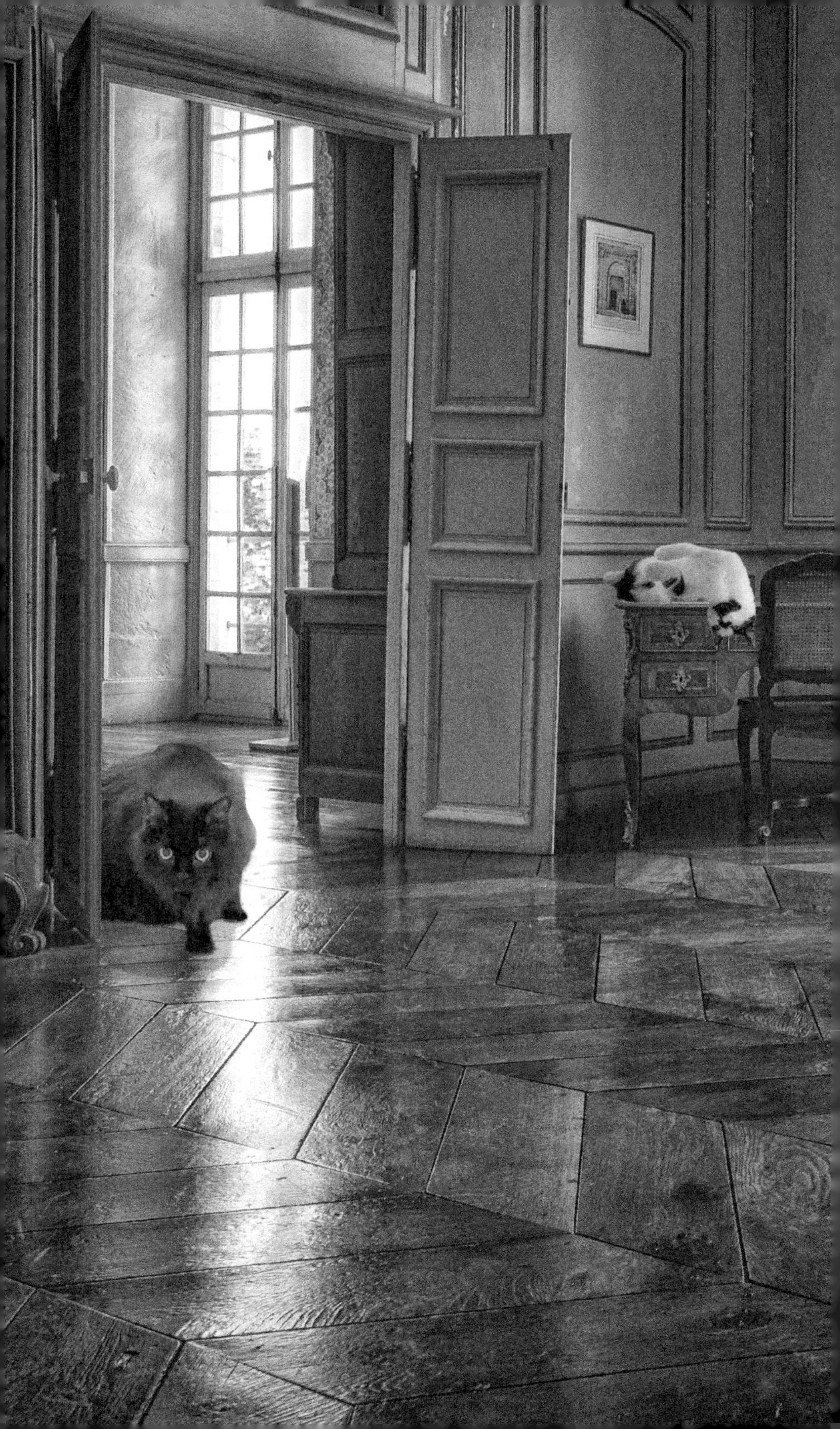

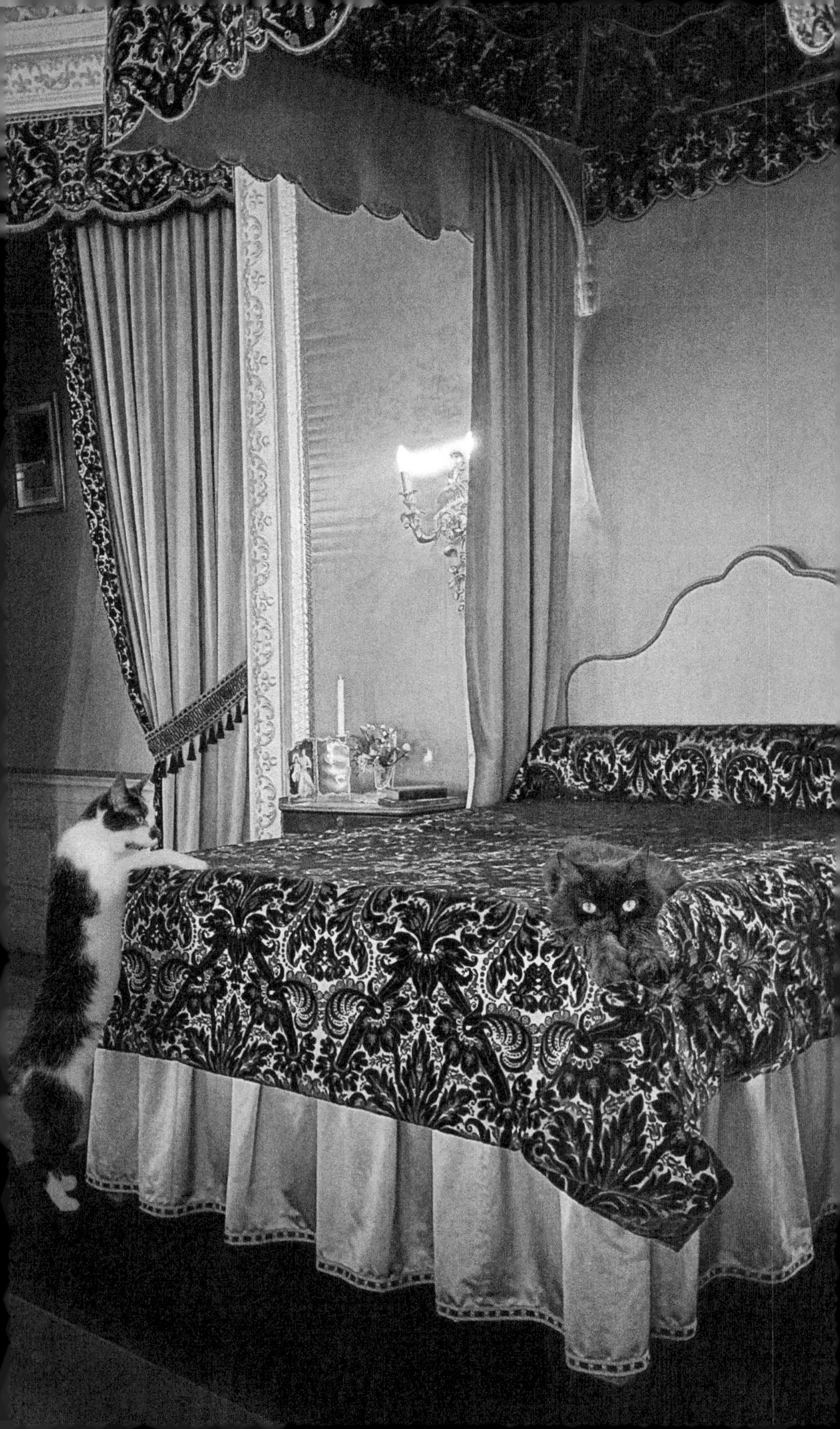

Chapter 7

Movement. A sliver of light. Clanging from the eating gallery. *"Fooood!"* A *crack*, a *creeeak*, and the *clinking* of metal on glass. A simpering Simpleton bounding down the hall. If anyone needs more proof of Pavlov's mindless mutt theory, they needn't look any further.

Yaaawwwnnn.

Streeetch.

Sleeeep.

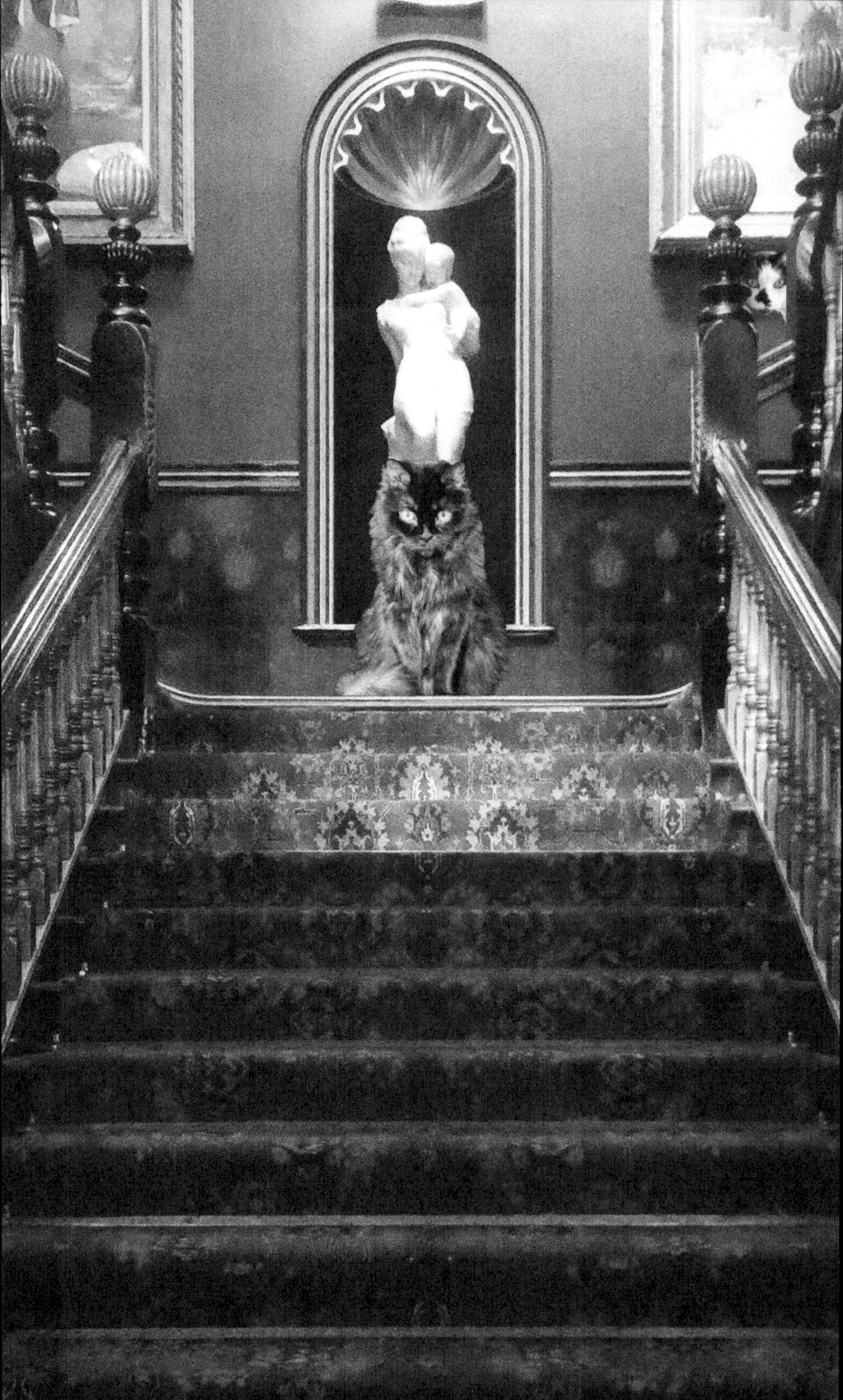

Chapter 8

Beneath me, an ocean of green fabric. Above me, a twister of flying vermin. Before me, a dog's open jaw with teeth bared telling me how beautiful I am in human speak. I try to run but the cloth bunches up underfoot. A net envelops me. The humans dance on all fours nearly stepping on my Beautiful Tail. Metal elephants crash into each other, their honking building to a deafening crescendo. The dragon approaches overhead swooping ever closer whilst casting shadow demons all around, fiery eyes locked onto their target. The Simpleton appears beside me within the net shaking uncontrollably with fear repeating "who's a good boy, who's a good boy, who's a good boy, hoozagooboi, hoozagooboi, hoozagooboi." The white giant's hand reaches through the net with long metal fingers and I hiss and scratch and sink my fangs into the fingers that come loose and become crinkled plastic. The dragon attacks and sinks her talons into me and lifts me up, the net disintegrating. The humans and the Simpleton watch from below silently as I'm taken high into the sky, the dragon's eyes blazing. But now I am the dragon, and she is in my claws, and I'm flying faster and higher. My castle is just ahead. In the valley below, dogs yelp from the rooftops and are trying to run for cover. But there is no escape. I take a giant breath and let forth an annihilating roar that levels the entire town and all dogs in existence, the world ablaze as its gets brighter, brighter, brighter...

 My eyelids part. A ray of light is shining into my eyes through a space in the bed frame above. I squint them closed. Muted mumblings echo beyond the sleeping quarters. I lengthen and let a giant sigh flow through my heavy limbs. I can't move, my limbs feel so heavy. They're as concrete as this damned - oh, right, different castle. I consider a quick post-sleep nap, but realize I am starving and require sustenance. I stand and reach my front legs out and drop my chest to the floor, then extend my chest forward as I stretch out my hind legs, first the right then the left. I lie back down and debate the pros and cons of going back to sleep. I can sleep or I can eat. If I sleep, then I am sleeping, and that is a glorious thing. But if I eat, then I am eating and that too be glorious. I do this for quite some time - minutes, hours, who could tell - and I decide I prefer the latter, so I stagger to the eating gallery. The floor feels softer than the usual cursed concrete and I am reminded that the servants finally heeded my demands for actual flooring, as if that's something that even needs consideration. Dimwits.

The dragon's eye shines boastfully into my new castle, insisting upon itself as the day's victor. It cuts arrogant beams of light through a jungle of boxes and barricades, casting shadows on the wall. There is much to do in this new dwelling, many battles to be waged and fought, various corners to rub up against and claim ownership over, many inspections to undertake and hiding places to investigate. But first, nom-noms.

As I suspected, the servants woke early and hunted for the day's provisions, though my bowl is oddly half-empty. I glare at the Simpleton licking its chops from outside the water chamber, surely waiting for its master to ask it who is a "good boy." *They don't mean you, you brainless bag of bolts!* If Picasso painted an impression of a panda, where nothing goes where it should on a beast of black and white, you might get an idea of what the Simpleton looks like. I would expound on its visage but I'm now eating and don't want to vomit as the rug is nowhere near.

I hear a door closing down the hall, followed by the Simpleton's growing cries. Now that I've quenched my thirst from the fountain, I go to a visible spot to scowl and judge the event. *Simpleton, you are nearly as disturbing to my ears as you are to my eyes, and that's saying a lot.* The servant exits the water chamber and responds to the Simpleton's wails. I increase the volume of my scowl. *Don't encourage the fool, Dimwit.* They approach me as I walk toward them, my head and Beautiful Tail high.

Good morrow, dutiful ward. I say, how fare thee? My Beautiful Tail in a question mark is also curious.

"Yes, My Queen. I hope you enjoy your new home and that it's enough to make up for our foiled mutinous quest." They reach down to caress the royal mane and I allow it. I rub my cheek on their leg followed by the rest of my body and every inch of my Beautiful Tail.

I follow them as they head to the front room. I leap onto my couch and begin to bathe myself with my tongue and the rays of the dragon's eye sun and watch as the servant removes items from green stones to place about the castle. In the bright light of mid-day, I can see this dwelling is much bigger than the last, with more space for me to expand my Queendom and keep the Simpleton at bay, and more windows so that I can better surveil the townspeople, shiny rumbling elephants, and flying vermin. The servant notices my supervision and offers pettings in appreciation. My breath slows and deepens into a low, rumbling purr that churns the burden of remembrances. The servant smiles and asks, "Do you like your new home, Queen Shosho?"

They're not so bad, you know, the humans. Despite their many faults, their limited intellect, clumsy stumps and mutinous pursuits, having them around is, dare I say it, not always disagreeable. I look into this one's face, kind, caring, as gentle fingers find the place behind my ear I can't reach. My simple servant, my humble human, my furless friend. I blink slowly in response.

A fatigue begins to set in. All this supervising is hard work indeed. I squint into the smug sunlight and beyond. Through the windows I spy fluffy-tailed vermin skittering across ropes and wires and the odd flying rat swooping sarcastically by. The Simpleton darts frantically at them, as if it would know what to do if successful. Does it even know we've overtaken a new castle? Well, simple things amuse Simpletons, so perhaps there's comfort that some things never change. *MEOW,* but that was indeed a large rat that just flew by! The Simpleton's too slow! 'Tis a job for a proper huntress! I leap off the couch to jump up the window.

Take *that,* and *that!* O, what a vicious warrior I am, determined to secure dinner for myself and perhaps for others if there's any left. I will get it, I will kill it and - where is it? Hmph, it's gone. Flown out of sight. I scan the sky left and right. Up there? No? No. Over there? No? No. *Bah, get thee away, Simpleton.* It's bounding and springing way too close for my liking. *You're too stupid to hunt for the house! Go find a servant to slobber over.* Grungy mongrel. I make way for the sleeping quarters, far from industrious Dimwits and springy Simpletons, and stretch out along the bed. A queen's work is never done.

...

I am stirred awake by a shuffle. A kerfuffle! An upheaval? Cat the catapult! O, no, 'tis just the servant hammering at the wall. Perhaps they are killing a sprite! I slant my ears back but stay wide-eyed. *I say, that is admirable work, ward, but do keep it down.* Dimwits.

I yawn and readjust my head and stretch out my feetsies. What's this? A warmth beside me. The heating apparatus? I feel it rise and fall beneath my hind legs as if breathing. But the heating apparatus doth not breathe! Blast! 'Tis the Simpleton, stealing my own body's heat! It looks up at me with tired, weary eyes, ears slanted sideways ready for my retaliation. I consider it for a moment. But my exhaustion runs deep, and any energy expended in admonishment would be borrowed from the next nap which is sorely needed. I yawn grandly. The servant completes the upkeep of my sleeping quarters and departs, dousing the torch. The Simpleton, still on guard, stiffens and prepares for the clash. But none shall come today. We've both had a tough go of it. Perhaps the Simpleton deserves a respite, as much as I deserve a little extra heat. I contemplate my options and decide to choose none. Be that adversity makes strange bedfellows, so we find ourselves paired, and so it goes.

    I turn my head in Kodi's direction without meeting his eyes, giving permission to rest. He relaxes his pose, curls his head into his little body and tucks his front paws beneath his chin. My jester's breathing is rhythmic, his purring, sonic, and at once, he is not entirely aggravating. I stretch languidly, my hind legs finding warmth beneath his furry, purring frame. Before putting my head down to sleep again, I narrow my eyes and flit my right ear at him. *Sniff my butt and you're dead.*

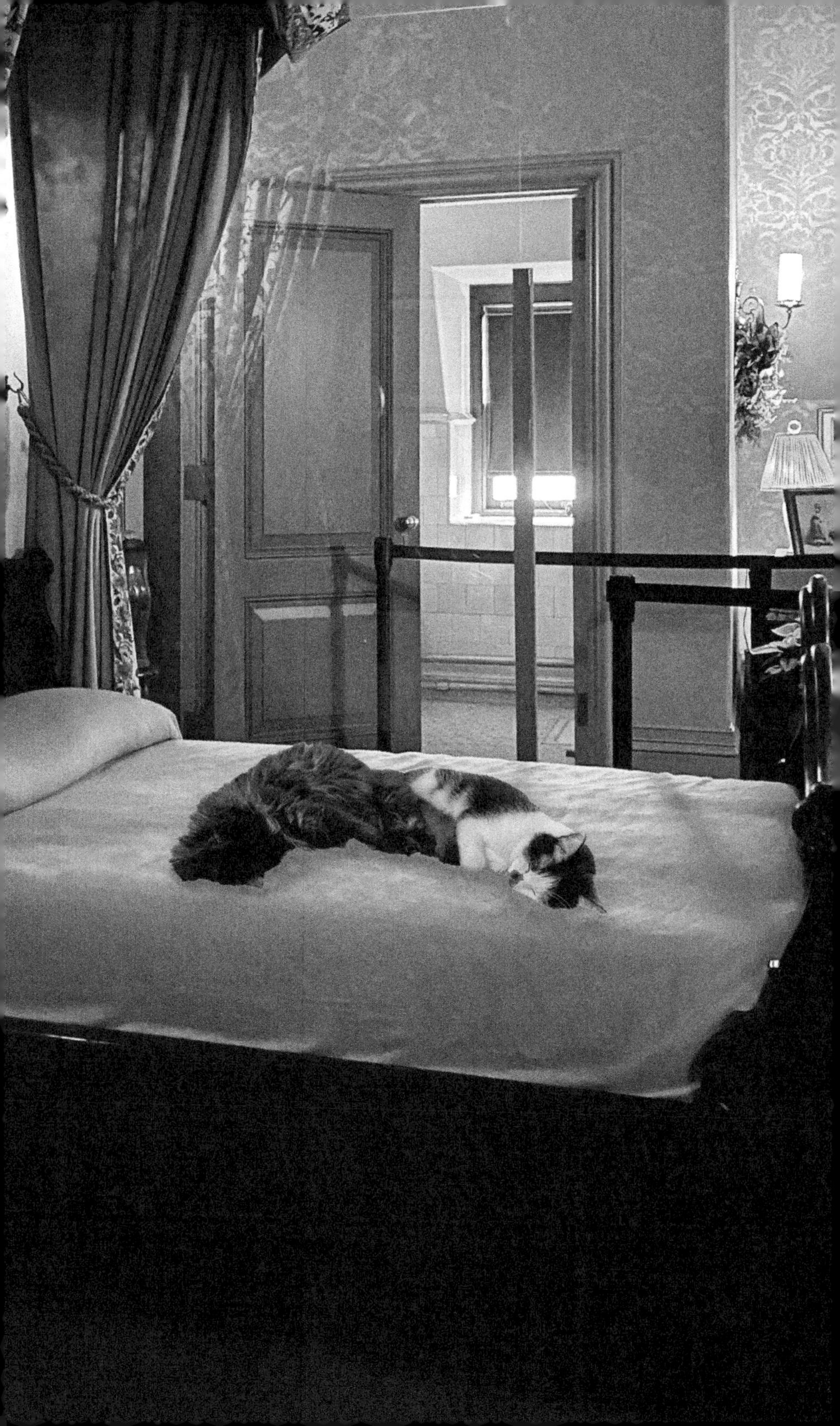

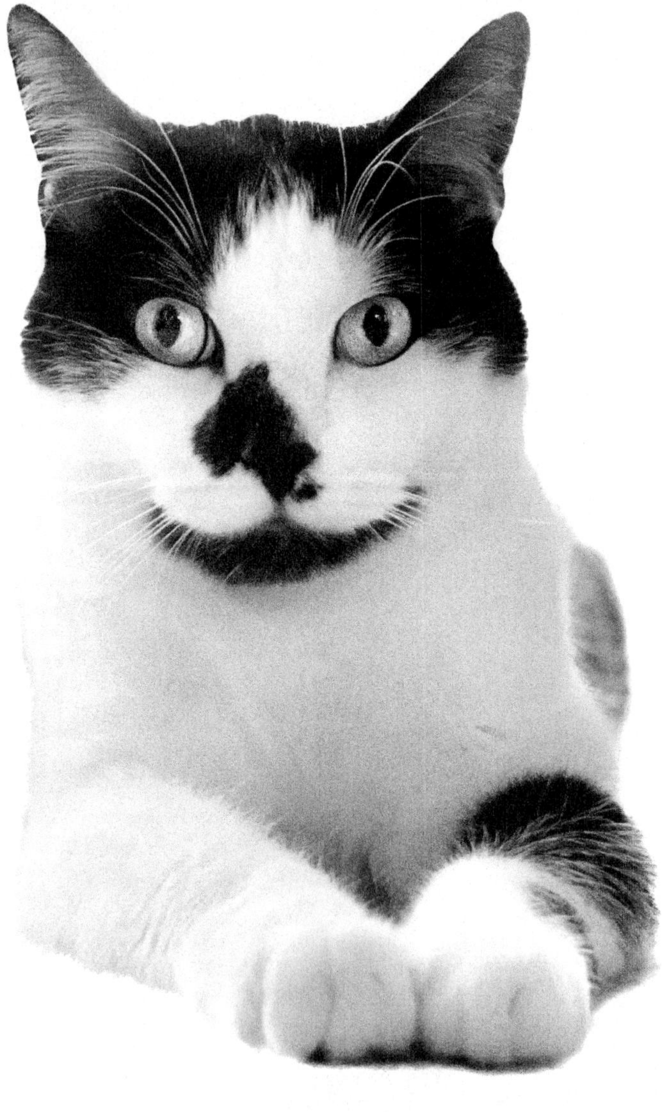

The Book of Kodi

So we moved. It was alright. Shorty was SUCH a drama queen. But what else is new. She got to play in the unpacked boxes where she could be all, "I'm queen and you're stupid," and blah blah. She's kind of a weirdo, but she's so pretty and I wish we cuddled more.

I didn't really like being in the carrier, but then I got cuddles and a brand new home with lots of fun places to jump and run and explore, and I also got cuddles and treats and some new toys as well as cuddles and then OH I almost forgot I got to go outside for the first time and that was fun until daddy put a harness on me cuz I like to jump and run and explore, but then after that I got cuddles and treats and then you know what else I got cuddles! All in all, it was great because, hoozagooboi? I am! Can we cuddle now?

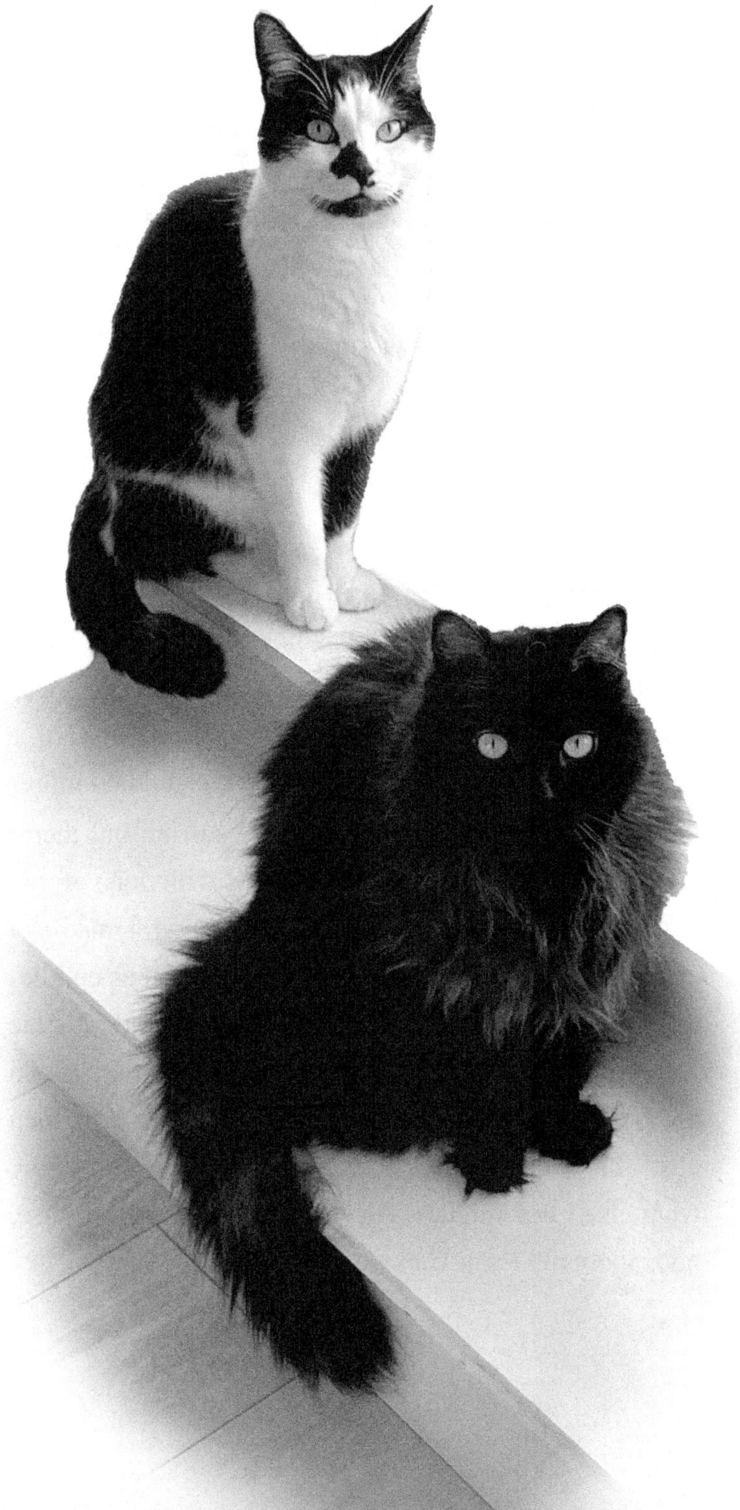

The Book of Fur Fiction

Inspired by the universe of Shorty and Kodi, some fans offered to write their own short stories and poems. The writers range greatly in age, background, and first language, but followers will recognize familiar elements in each of these works. I hope you enjoy reading them as much as I have. If you would like to contribute a story for a future edition, please send your submission to me at shortyandkodi@gmail.com.

Peace and purrs out,

Rob

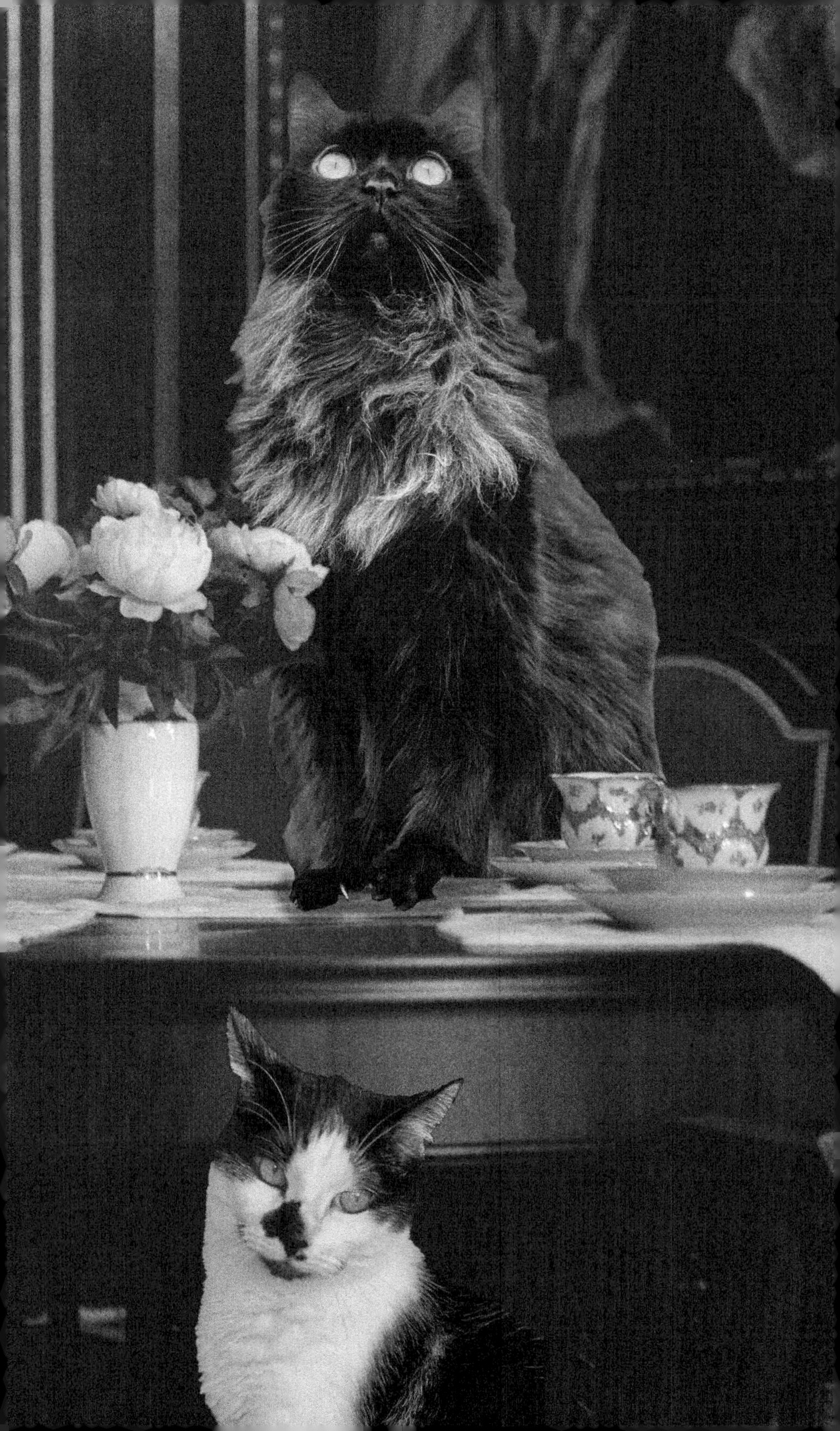

The Realization of The Royal Queen

By Miss Josh Emmett

I sit proudly gazing at myself in the royal mirror. I am The Queen. I have regal pointed ears as a crown. And, oh my stars, I do wear gorgeous fluff. *What? I think. What is this upon my fluff? My gorgeous dark fluff? White? Gray? Oh, my stars and garters! A pox on it! GO AWAY!* I command. I hath yelled that last command aloud as a deep voice says, "Shorty? I'm busy. Fix it yourself." I do. I am The Queen. I scratch the door until the form appears that owns the deep voice and opens the door with a resigned sigh.

Thus, I am here on the Royal Balcony. I hath found a warm patch of sun, rolled over on my back and am warming my lovely fluff. I was born a queen, my mother said so. (Well, I couldn't hear it at the time, but as soon as my ears opened, she told me I was a very loud demanding queen. And, yes, later I discovered that all female felines are queens and males are toms, but I set about correcting that concerning myself.) She taught me to be always clean, hold my head and tail high, walk like a lady and tone my meow down. And then she was gone. All who were like me were gone and I found myself with two tall creatures walking on their back legs. I was in a large palace and feeling a bit small. Of course, I was but a kitten at the time. I took care of that by diligently practicing climbing, spider walking, arching and hissing. I can roll like no other queen. So, I crown myself The Queen and take over the palace. I am sure *they* were not expecting to be trained so well. But they call me Shorty, not Queen. And, worst of all, they brought home a tom and called it Kodi. But they never stop... ShoSho, KoKo, ShoShobeans, KoKobeans, Hoozagoboi... oh, my royal stars.

    I have a large kingdom known as Canada. I have ruled from three of my palaces, so far. I know this because I am very intelligent and I watch a screen with all my subjects on it who appear to be quite small. Well, all the better for me; two tall beings are quite enough. I do also hath the tom to deal with after all. The tall ones call each other Bryan, who I have trained to give excellent pats and scritches and rubs, and Rob, who is a 5-star Michelin chef and takes me in the Royal Carriage, ensconced in the safety box, to people called Vets (whom I assume are to make sure The Queen is in good health at all times but those tall creatures touch me in very unroyal places and poke me with sharp pointy thingies. Well, I hath left my royal mark on more than one of those and Bryan cries about it... oh, he said he cries about me. Me? I shall never be unhealthy! I have decreed it.) Plus, Servant Rob is also my Royal Photographer. I keep him quite busy, as I fancy I could have been quite the actress had I not become The Queen. Step aside Dame Helen Mirren!

Hmm... a bit of shift with the sun.

Where was I? Ah, yes. My life as The Queen. I have seen another Queen in the Kingdom of England who calls herself: Her Majesty Queen Elizabeth II of Great Britain. Two can play that game. I call myself: Her Majesty Queen Shorty Shoshobeans I of The Commonwealth of Canada. Now, I am not sure, but Her Royal Highness seems to have an overabundance of Jesters. I have enough problems with one! One day I caught him playing with a tasty live morsel out here on the Royal Balcony. It was time to go in. I got up, passed him, ate the moth, and went in. (I am sure he had a sad look on his face. Silly thing thought he had a new ally, but I defeated it forthwith... and it tasted good too.) Another time, there was - and I am a bit ashamed to admit this, so I blame it on the servants - there was a crack in the royal balcony wall and the Bit of Silliness went through it into a secret chamber, so that I had to make Servant Rob retrieve the scoundrel and then I had to punish him with the torture harness. So, to cheer him up, I allowed him back on the royal balcony and knighted him. 'Tis a small thing, I can rescind it when I please, and it sounds rather hilarious: Sir Kodi Hoozagooboi Kokobeans, Jester of the Royal Court of The Commonwealth of Canada.

I needed the chuckle and moved my fluff again.

But back to why I demanded privacy upon the Royal Balcony. First, the servants noticed I was having a bit of a *very* small problem jumping onto their sleeping place and bought me... oh, even to think of it gives me the royal shivers... my own little Royal Staircase. The shame of it all. And now this. Oh, the worst of the worst. Woe is me. I have found *white and gray* hairs in my fluff! There. I said it. Aloud, it appears, as Servant Rob just asked if I wanted to come in.

I went in and climbed into my Royal Cardboard Chamber. I, of course, have several. They are strong and keep me safe. I know as I evaluate them often, day and night. One night, Servant Rob threw me out! How dare he? The humiliation. The sorrow. The pain. I must admit that I, The Queen, sought solace in the warmth of my Knight. Oh, do not judge me. I was once filmed holding hands, in a moment of sadness, with Servant Bryan. Some horrid paparazzi even put it on the screen! Have they no decency! Yet, I am not ashamed and hold my head high. One must expect betrayal in my position. However, if I ever find out who it was, I shall put him in the torture harness and keep him there forever! OFF WITH HIS HEAD! No, a Queen is *never* overdramatic but must rule with a stern paw and I truly believe 'twas the Jester.

Sadly, I saw on the screen that my dear friend, Elizabeth II, crossed over the Royal Rainbow Bridge. And I discovered that she, too, had a little Royal Staircase and her fur, of course, was a lovely white. And so it goes: As I went for pat-pats and stroking with Servant Rob, I pointed out to him that I needed my royal staircase to get to the seat of *his* chair. And I shall continue to rule, as I have comforted myself with the thought that I have several Royal Lives left. I have ruled Kingdom Canada for a goodly amount of time so far and, like Elizabeth II, Shorty I shall rule a long time accepting all the small comforts that we Queens deserve.

PRRBBT

(Royal Signature of Shorty I)

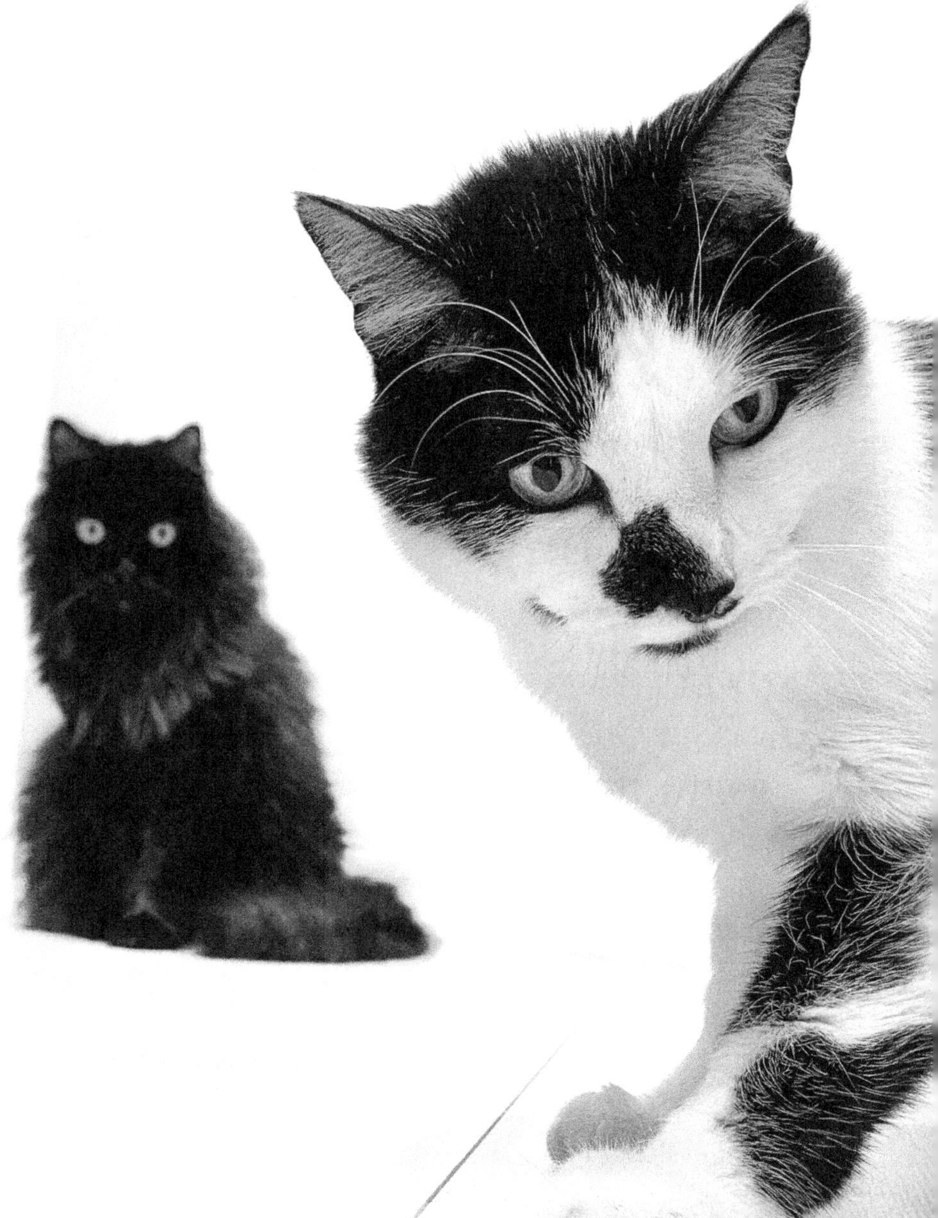

Three Thoughts of One Activity

By Briana M. Miles

Queen Shorty:

My humble knave stands erect,
For his daily ritual he is ready,
It becomes wise to thus expect
A weird performance most zany.

He thinks himself adroit,
With the exotic dance of his kin,
He knows not his performance is spoilt
By thine frame housing his soul within

Still, his devoted dance is not without merit,
As my Tail bestows him my favor.

This done allows the knave to inherit
To his life a renewed fervor.

Performance done, I take my leave,
Showing what beauty true grace can weave.

Kodi the Jester:

The Queen, I must confess,
Moves gracefully without fuss or mess,
But when the servant contorts
I can always retort
That I can charm him the best!

Robert the servant

Whether skull crushers or warrior poses are done
Working out with my cats is definitely twice the fun!

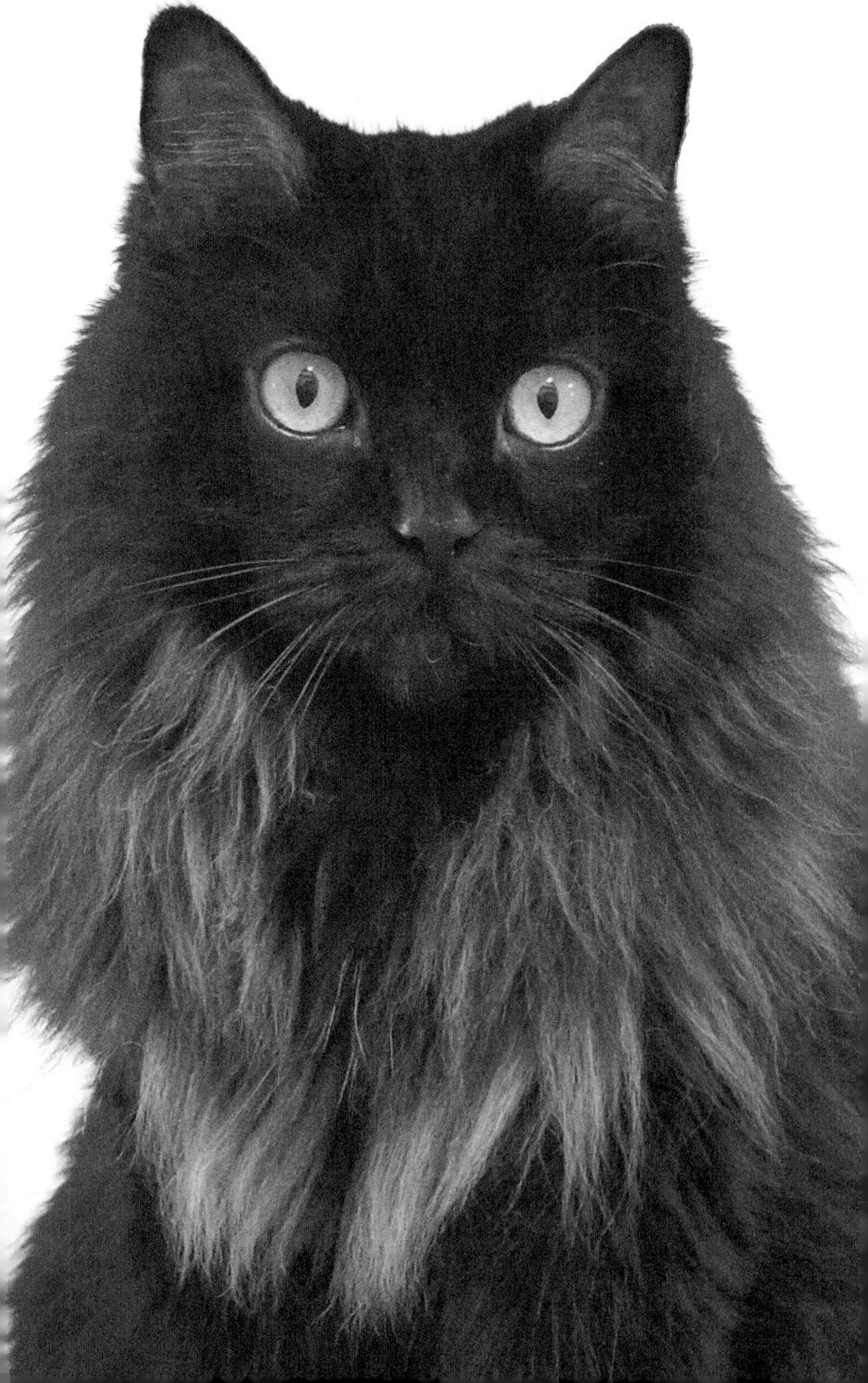

Hiss Me Deadly

By Eileen R. Golden

She wasn't like the other skirts who hung around Rob's Place, all big blondes with curves till next week and lipstick red as a man's stab wound to the chest. They'd hold your hand, pretend like they cared. Then after they'd gotten all they wanted, the claws came out.

The brunette was different. Wrapped up in a black fur coat, she had big round eyes that could look right through you, through the wall behind you and all the way back to your apartment to the wallet you'd forgotten, as usual, on the dresser, and could count every bill inside while sizing you up to see if you could buy her a martini with what little change you had in the pocket of your second-hand trousers.

She wasn't picky, in other words.

I grabbed a handful of nuts from the dish Rob had set out earlier, and kept an eye on the doll as she sauntered across the floor and graced me with a bored glance over one shoulder. Suddenly her eyes went rattlesnake wild and she lunged at me with nails out, nails as long and sharp as stiletto blades. "MRRRROWWWWW!!!!!"

Afterward, as I was studying my new reason for avoiding broads that had just been carved across my upper lip - studying it in my reflection (the brass rail footrest that ran along the bottom of the bar was very shiny indeed) - Rob pointed out that the dame considered that bowl of nuts to be HER dish, and "don't nobody better eat outta her dish, Mr. Kodi. Not nobody."

He was swell, all right. He should have warned me, but then, Hitler should have stayed out of Smolensk, too. Should-haves didn't amount to a tray of dead butts, not in this world - or the next.

I dragged myself back upright and pressed my handkerchief against the wound. It was still bleeding a little. I looked at the handkerchief again, and thought of the war, of the girl in Paris, the French girl in that dive in Paris who'd given it to me. What was she doing tonight? Sighing, I let myself out into the rainy evening.

Then I remembered that I'm a cat, and we hate rain. I sighed again. It was going to be a long, long night.

Me, Your Majestic Highness

By SnowRainStella

Behold the view of my Majestic Tail
This is My Queendom from where I hail

The Queendom flourish in my charismatic paws
Intruders meet with swift swords and sharp claws

None can sit in the fortress of Thy Queen
So exceptional am I, with a befitting sheen

The castle stands tall on the gates of hell
Demons pour out with intentions not well

Thumps and Thwacks, a fierce battle ensues
They try to escape, but I never lose

I lunge forward like hundreds of dragons
The hell beast screams under my talons

Mmaaaw the roar heard trembles the beast
My dangerous leap pin down the meek

Foolish and stupid may you be
Benevolent mercy I bestow to thee

Mrrp prrbbtts, the mercy I gave
Be thee grateful for my mighty grace

Though you're insolent and refuse to be trained
Thy Queen will rule with the fiercest of face.

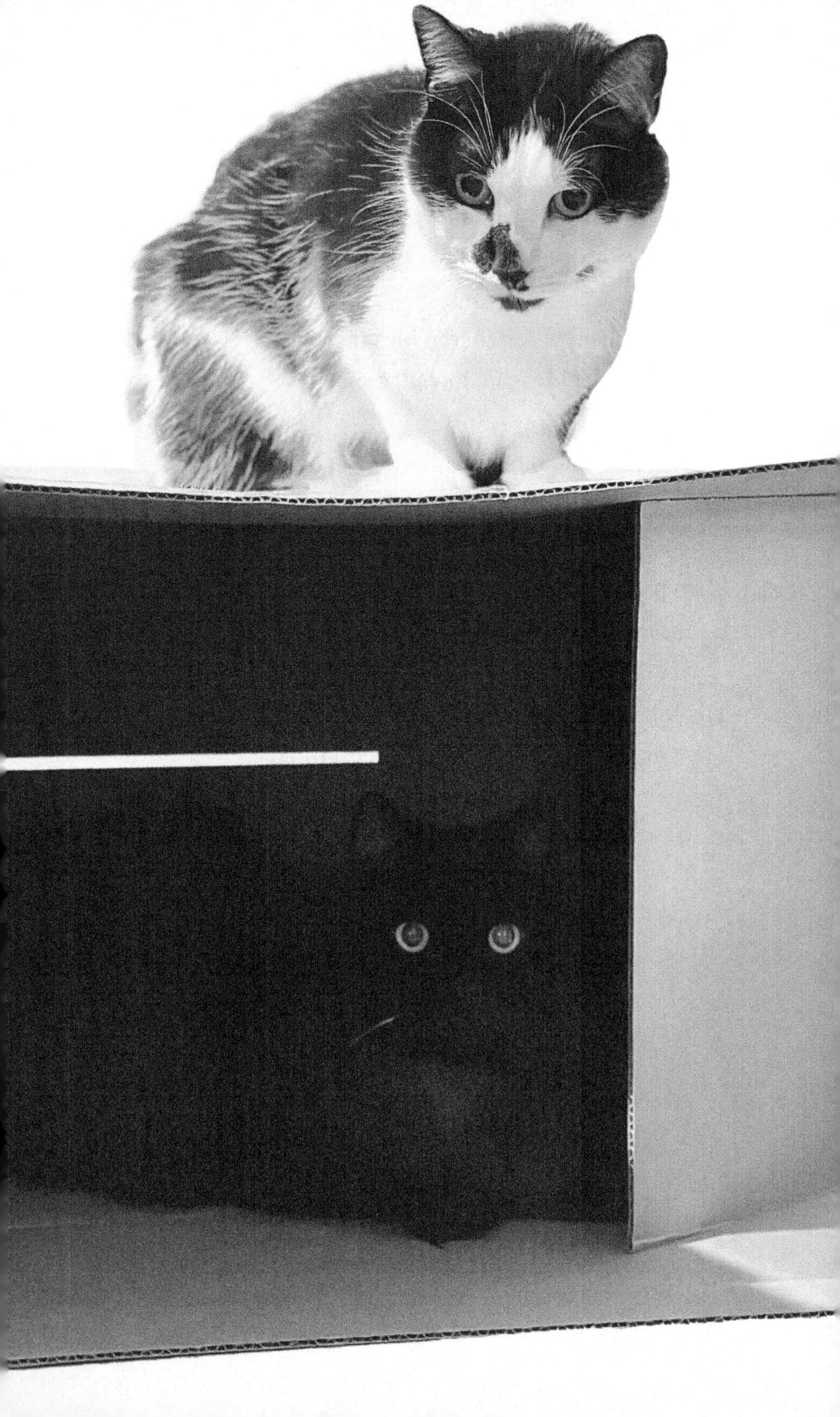

Queen and the Hell Gate

By SnowRainStella

It is a morning like any other, with birds chirping and perching outside. A gorgeous black beauty with lustrous fur can be seen laying on the coach. The queen of the royal palace was taking a nap. As her giant and strong but slow and dimwitted servant passes by, the queen slowly opens her eyes to show her lemon yellow eyes. She takes a yawn and shows her long and sharp teeth that could cut the thickest of flesh like water.

"It was a great night yesterday... but nothing can beat a refreshing nap on the lavish royal coach." She proceeds to sit up and shake her majestic fur.

"Look at this mess. Let me groom my tail back to its majestic and charming form, befitting for my marvelous self. I have a face and position to maintain." The black beauty proceeds to groom her tail with such dignity that her surroundings start to fade in front of her. No eyes can get over her eloquent movements. "Now then, where might that Simpleton could be?" The black beauty, done with her grooming, jumps down from the coach.

"It's now time for my royal snacks. Let's take a stroll of my lavish and royal queendom." The great beauty walks to the large glass window. The sunlight coming through the window fell on Her Highness's black lush fur making it shine like thousands of diamonds embroidered on her ebony coat. "One of the few things that remind me of my royal self from the past."

The queen lies down in front of the large window as she let herself soak in the beaming sunlight.

"There are no royal musicians that can please my great and sensitive ears and earn my grace, nor even come close to deserve to reside in my mighty presence. No, none worth it, but this."

Her Royal Highness always loved the voices of nature and the best of music it can offer.

Yes.

The majestic black cat that stands out alone in every environment is the reincarnation of the great, invincible Queen Alexandria Shubert Vespertine. She ruled more than half the land in another dimension which has never been known as a land for the weak.

It was a land where dragons, demons, evil spirits and dinosaurs roamed even till the moment Empress Alexandria took her last breath. Even the weakest of humankind and smallest of creatures were known to possess the abilities, known to us humankind of this dimension, as magic.

The almighty Empress Alexandria was the strongest queen that won over and united several lands and brought up a nation that was named after the golden era it showed to humankind.

But alas, as if destiny playing a melancholic song, the undefeated queen was forced to take her last breath because of an unforeseen illness.

But God had another plan for Alexandria the Great as she rebirthed in the body of a cat in this dimension with her memories from her previous life intact.

It took her long to get used to the strange dimension and its rules, but she soon conquered her now palace and queendom after she forced her dimwitted servant to submit before her and forfeit all his then and future possessions over to her.

Now she is the queen of her royal palace, though it is not to her liking and it will never be able to meet her standards. But she refused to leave this home and look for another one when our benevolent queen found a massive danger lurking towards the humankind of this dimension.

Since then, she has been sacrificing her precious naps and luxuries she deserves for the sake of her dimwitted servant and her simpleton tenant.

"Last night may not compare to the royal huntings of my previous life, but it was indeed more ecstatic and exhilarating than the previous nights."

After a while, the giant servant once again passes by the queen, but this time he makes some weird sound.

"Must you disturb my costly and precious quality time? This dimwit and sluggish servant just can't learn to behave himself in my royal presence and keeps embarrassing me with his weird and insolent antics."

As beautiful and majestic as she can be, the empress starts to groom herself and her tail once again.

"I wish to spend some more of my precious time listening to the nature's voice but I have this dimwit and that simpleton to take care of. Alas, being a queen of such incompetent subjects is such a tedious duty for my majestic self. These insolent beings fool around all the time, unaware of my mighty duties that I must perform for the sake of my queendom, even at the cost of sacrificing my leisure time and cherished naps.

"I believe it's time, I shall take my leave now. But fret not, for I shall provide you with the opportunity to serve and please me sometime again."

The majestic queen rises and heads for her fortress. As she draws closer, she sees a white cat with black patches much smaller than her majestic self dash out her fortress opening.

"Again?!"

The queen hisses at the meek cat in front of her.

"How often do I need to warn you before you take heed of my words, you fool!"

"But I just wanted to see it once again!"

"Silence, you dumb child. Don't you know what they say? Curiosity kills the cat. I never brought you up to be my soldier. My mighty self can amount to more than a battalion of dragons. I have no need for you here."

"But you said I can jump high and that you will train me and turn me into your general!"

The white cat had finally spoken up for himself, but it felt like a child throwing a tantrum.

"Quit acting like a brat. You don't have enough patience needed for a soldier and can't even follow my orders with utmost sincerity yet. How dare you enter my fortress without your queen's permission? I will never grant a simpleton like you permission to fight by my side ever. Heed my words and stay out of this fortress that rest over the gates of hell, unless you wish to be corrupted like all those heinous criminals outside my safe and heavenly palace."

The queen casually walks inside her fortress.

"But, please, give me a chance to prove myself!"

"Don't you dare talk back to your queen. This queendom is under my sovereignty. If you don't want your demise from the hands of hell dwellers, don't take a step closer. You can't survive in this stronghold of a fortress unless I teach you, and I shall not."

Those was her last words before immersing herself in her own thoughts.

"That dimwit servant, no matter how much I order him to, he doesn't remember to put a gate and a guard on the fortress. Must the queen do everything by herself? Were I in my previous life, any order I had given would have been done right that instant. Alas, I should never have shown that simpleton what goes on inside this fortress."

A few years prior, when the servant brought her the weak and powerless white kitty, she took pity and mercifully took him under her mighty wing. She cherished him and raised him. But he was a simple and ignorant youngster to say the least.

But the same simpleton grew up to possess the physical attributes of a warrior.

Once the naive child asked her about the mysterious fortress and her incomprehensible actions within. The empress answered him with pure honesty but he got stubborn and demanded to witness it all for himself. Her heart overflowing with ecstasy and love and pride for her grown-up tenant, she agreed and even promised to make a soldier out of him and have him fight by her side against evil beings.

Little did the empress know it would all turn into her biggest regret.

"Come my child, let your queen grant you with the blessed eyes," she said as she groomed the kitten and bestowed upon him with the blessed eyes and ears, making him able to see and hear what others couldn't before taking him with her to her forbidden fortress.

There the youngling saw a fierce battle between his almighty queen and the scariest of hell beings. In his excitement, the foolhardy cat jumped in the fortress mid-battle but found himself to be overwhelmed by monstrous thoughts, only to be saved by our queen who slayed all the evil spirits trying to possess the child.

From then on, the queen never let her subjects get near danger, howsoever stupid, insolent and incompetent they may be. She refused to provide her simpleton subject with the blessed eyes and ears ever again.

"This fortress is getting older and weaker. I should order the dimwit to bring me a new one, hopefully with a gate to keep out that simpleton," said the queen while clawing at the walls of her fortress. "Now shall the queen polish her unmatched hunting skills?"

She takes a leap that measures the wall. Suddenly, the difference in size between her and the fortress starts to shrink to nothing. She lands back on the ground with a loud thump. Her tail crashes in the walls with a thundering sound. *Thwack. Thump, thump, thwack.*

The majestic empress is filled with ecstasy after the last night of battle to say the least. She looks forward to the coming night.

"Come if you dare to face this fierce queen. I shall be prepared to greet you all with my fearsome teeth and dagger-like claws."

After hours pass by, the night falls once again.

The dimwit is asleep and the simpleton is sulking elsewhere by himself.

In the dark room, the darker and majestic queen cat enters. But her eyes are different. There is a glow in the eyes of the great queen; they seem almost holy. She can see and hear what others can't even fathom with her blessed eyes and ears.

She makes her way through the room towards her fortress. She can hear it clearly. The hell gates are opening again. There is a white, blue and yellow light swirling around a pitch black spot in the middle of her fortress. It was as black as a black hole. No one can see or assume its depth.

"This is nothing more than a mere playground for me, the almighty and invincible Queen Alexandria the Great! Come how many of you may. Come one by one or all together, I will greet you all the same and bestow on you the same fate your predecessors have earned from me!"

The lonesome majestic creature roars.

Mwaaaaah!

Suddenly, a pitch black shadow pops out of the abyss. If not for its two droopy red eyes and a gaping mouth, it would have looked like the chasm was floating up from the floor.

But the queen lunges towards the spectre. She lands across the hole with the evil spirit under her claws. She slices at it and it evaporates. Three more hell dwellers try to escape through the passage but get thrashed into the fortress wall by the mighty power of the queen's tail.

The empress turns around and sees an evil spirit trying to climb over and out of her fortress.

"Don't assume you can escape from my royal grasp, you lowly creature of the hell." She takes a leap and stabs the spirit with her claw and drags it down with her weight.

"This great queen will show you all what it feels like to fight against the invincible queen. Consider it an honor of the highest might!"

The battle continues as more spirits continue pouring out of the hell gate in the middle of the fortress. In the end, after hours of battle, the demons stop coming out and the hell gate starts to shrink. It closes, finally.

"Fun indeed. Something akin to my royal huntings does exist in this world of weak beings. I am glad I chose this palace over others even though it is not up to my high principles and liking." The empress casually strolls out of her fortress after spending her time playing around with the toys of purgatory.

The queen's dimwit servant comes out of another room. As his eyes fell on Her Highness, he bends down and starts to make some weird noises while advancing his hands towards the queen.

"You insolent and foolish servants should be grateful and feel blessed for being able to lay your hands on my marvelous black fur and to be of my service. My subjects used to faint after receiving mere glances of me, that's how mighty I was and still am. But I allow you to provide me with your service and permit you to pet and massage me."

Years ago, when she first entered in the palace in the possession of her servant she subdued, she was immediately displeased by its low standards and decided to leave right after taking a small nap.

But in her dreams, the queen met with the gods who had granted her a new life. They told her about the evil spirits that escape from hell and possess all the other creatures on earth, causing them to either commit crimes or cut their life span. It was also these evil beings that took away the mighty queen's previous life.

They gave her a chance to exact revenge on those demons from the underworld that surface on the earth through her now servant's home. She possessed the almighty ability to purify and free someone from the influence of those spirits. She also purified her dimwit servant when she subdued him.

But the annoyed and upset queen refused to stay in the shabby palace and wished to leave immediately.

That's when the gods provided her the advantages of being able to hunt down the evil spirits and the ecstasy it provides. They also granted the mighty queen with the ability to hear angels and fairies singing in nature.

They said she will be granted with the highest honor and made the queen of heaven and hell once she completes this life span.

And finally, our queen accepted the offer with a benevolent heart.

Ever since, she has been protecting her queendom and her ignorant subjects along with the whole world around her palace with the fiercest of fist and face.

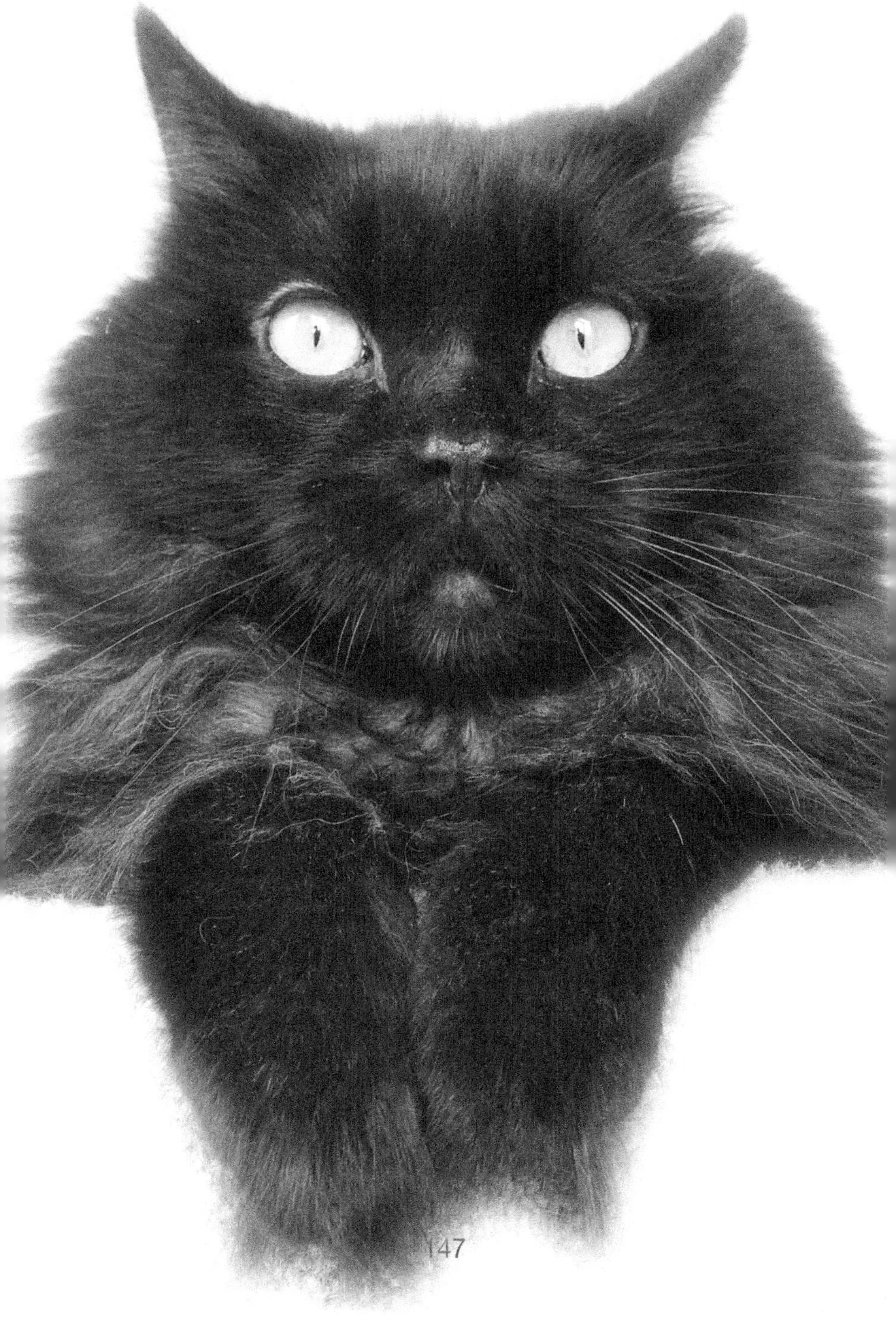

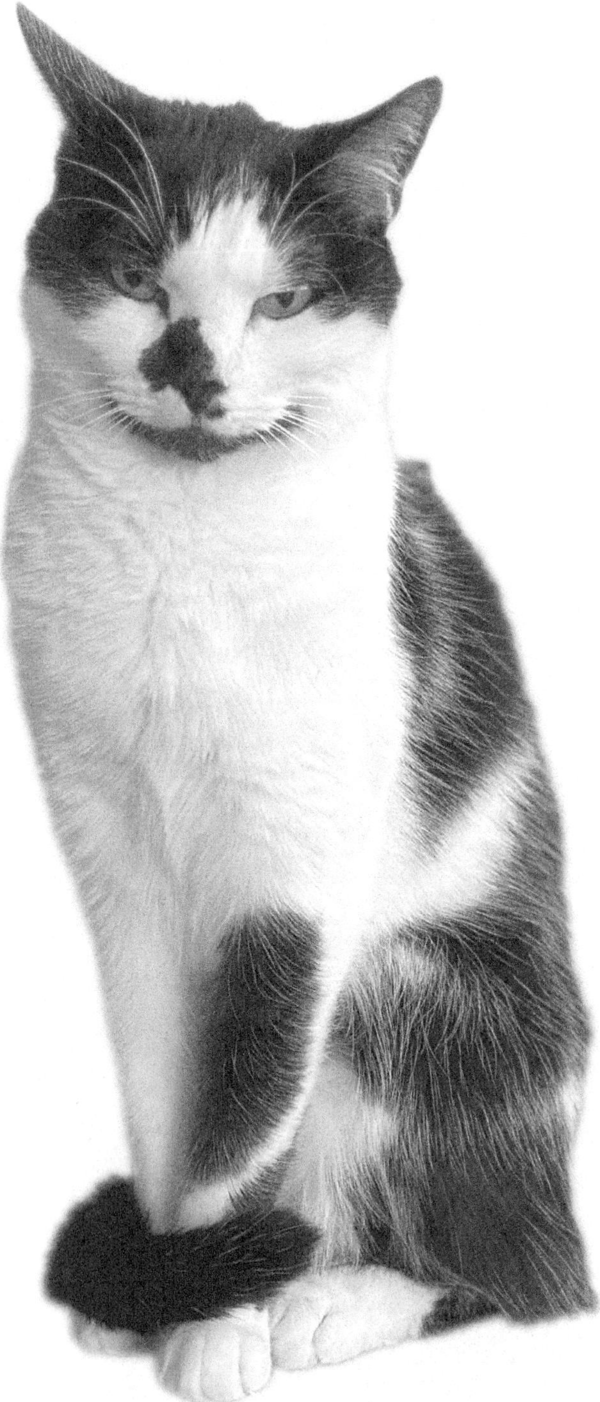

The Fool's Folly

By Amy Tracy

Startled awake, Shorty blinked slowly, wondering at the disruption. She was faced with a vision of grace, strength, and eyes so astoundingly beautiful and aware that one would be drawn immediately into their depths. She casually licked a paw acknowledging herself in the glass of the large window she had slumbered in front of. Usually, she would've been incensed at her sleep being disturbed, but as the sun had so impatiently moved on from her spot, she sheathed her claws and contemplated the source of the sound for a moment. She knew, of course, that she would find Him, breathing nearby, and considered unleashing her glorious murder mitts again. Her shadow in this life, her opposite, was never far from her side. In all ways, He was her opposite. Simple and spritely, downright gleeful at times, His very existence a mockery of everything a cat should be. She loathed him, and He loved her equally as much. He was painted like a clown, black patches covering his mostly white fur in silly shapes like he had knocked over an ink well and simply rolled in its contents. Even their coats seemed to speak of their inner nature. Hers was a decadent sable with a mantle that looked as though the sun had draped itself around her neck, lightening her liquid black to a warm gold.

He was always up to something unbecoming. There was a reason she was the Queen; aside from her majestic looks, she was born a ruler, a fighter, a divine gift. She only kept him around because his antics seemed to entertain the furless peasants. She ran an ordered queendom, and her mere voice brought delicacies and amusements. She only needed to croon to them, and they would lavish praise upon her. They would lay their bodies down on her dais, something they called a "couch," and allow her to practice the ancient fighting style of all cats. Purr an ominous rumble and punish them with her fuzzy dagger mitts of doom. It was essential to keep in fighting shape even though the queendom was living in a time of peace. There were still threats, birds, glasses on tables, and the ever-allusive tiny red light. Proper training was crucial and something the simple Good Boi did not understand. He was always running askance and freezing in these odd positions, tail (which was too long to be decent) straight up as though he believed these antics could protect the realm.

Now as she scanned the glorious expanse of her lands from high atop the window ledge, she could not see Him. Resigned to keeping the Fool alive, she let out a delicate chirp and stretched to her full immaculate length with the idea of searching him out and getting a well-deserved snack. The fading sunlight licked off her fuzzy boots as she jumped down, landing as gently as though she had been a leaf aloft on the breeze.

Using her perfect vision and laser focus, she scanned the room she was in for a glimpse of white and black. She assessed each area keenly aware that the Fool could often be found in a ridiculous tangle, asleep tucked up in a corner or on a furless peasant. She shook her mane in frustration, licked a paw in resignation, and proceeded further into the realm. She bent looking under the dais and found nothing. She reached the place of the throne and was happy not to find Him there. She continually had to tell him he wasn't allowed to sully it with his short white fur. She peered around in the potted forest in the corner and still hadn't located him. She was beginning to grow concerned, much to her disappointment. Typically he would not linger this far from her side, which, while irritating, had grown into a comfort. She licked another paw and chastised herself for being emotional; he was merely entertainment for the peasants, and she certainly did not care for him. Despite her inner monologue, her concern grew with the shadows lengthening through the realm. Before she knew it, she found herself chirping out to him. She looked up and down the length of the Great Hall, the space that the furless called the living room, and still could not see Him anywhere. She thought it was odd that he had ventured so far outside of her glorious aura and moved ever further into the depths of her lands.

Venturing into the sleeping quarters, she thought she would surely find him performing the rites. He was at least adept at anointing the freshly warmed "clothing" the furless wore to hide their skins, a sacred rite where their basic coverings were thoroughly coated with the fur of the highest beings. It was a gift that they relished and often lamented aloud about. Alas, there were no piles of folded cloth to anoint upon the sleeping platform and no fool atop them. Concern wrapped itself around her highness like the blanket of darkness in the chamber. She did a quick perusal under the bed and wardrobe, with nothing showing itself except a small contingent of the dust bunny army that kept peace in the lower realms. Nodding at their captain, who maintained their unmoving stoic stance, she retreated to the room's outer rim, considering where she ought to search next. To focus herself, she elected to leave a blessing for the furless and graciously rolled about on the soft bits they called "pillows." That good deed down, she was confident the clowder of goddesses would bless the rest of her mission.

She went canny out into the next part of the realm as fear of a more significant threat had taken the Fool (unaware, obviously) and did not wish to befall the same fate. She used her exceptional stealth mode, slipping around the corner with a mere whisper of fur against the castle wall. The space before her was wide open and lit by brilliant torches, so she would need to be quiet to avoid the threat she thought had now consumed the Fool. She was no longer on a mission of search and rescue but a holy mission of vengeance! Her eyes narrowed, and her breathing slowed, muscles solid in a pounce pose taught to her by her masters as a kitten; she scanned the open space with wariness.

She calculated the trajectory of the precise jump she would need to make to slip through unseen space. She saw the lines of space out before her as she planned the route. One stealthy jump to the side and another remarkably tricky even for one so skilled as her off the side of the "island" (which she didn't understand because thankfully there was no water). If correctly executed, she could traverse the wide-open area before her. She sat in absolute stillness as she had practiced knowing she needed to "be the darkness." She could not allow herself to be seen as this spot was clearly an easy attack point for whatever beast had taken the Fool. She centred herself in her mind settling further into Pounce Pose and allowing herself an internal smile at how cute the furless were when they practiced their own version of pounce meditation flow. They called it some cute nonsense word, yoga? As that thought flowed through her mind, she reminded herself this was ultimately for who she was on this journey. The furless peasants would be stricken without the Good Boi and his entertaining silliness.

Silent and composed within herself, she leaped. She landed quieter than a breath in the shadow of the grand island and kicked a back foot celebrating her amazingness. That's when she saw her next challenge. She locked in on the food bowl. A tantalizing mound of food sat in the center of her crystalline bowl, calling to her with the unrelenting seduction of a siren. She was so hungry now, and she was so close. The bowl was at the edge of the shadow in the beam of one of the torches taunting her. She wanted a snack even before she had performed her jumps of precision. She considered the folly of continuing the journey with only vengeance fuelling her and decided she needed to risk exposure in the light. Her tongue was raspier than ever, and she knew she might not have water again before this mission was complete. Slinking closer to the wafts of fish solidified her decision, and she found herself gorging on the sweet treat and then slaking her thirst from the bowl of clear water before she knew it. Replenished and ready to exact retribution, she pressed on stalwart to exact full-blown revenge! No matter how idiotic and irritating, the Fool was a part of her kingdom! And none shall escape her wrath for daring to harm any of her subjects!

    She raised her warrior head to the sky and strode through the kitchen's light, begging her foe to engage. She proudly strutted, knowing she was ready to throw paws and end this. As she proceeded through the wide-open killing field and no attack came, she felt the slimmest glimmer of hope the Fool was alive. She may have even hoped he was not gone forever, not that she would ever admit it. Shorty thought that if her enemy hadn't engaged with her this far into the realm, she would seek them out for an ultimate final battle in their chosen space. She scoffed as there was not a square inch of her queendom with which she was not intimately familiar. She'd lain at the very edges of this realm at the "Door" with not even so much as a whisker twitch of fear. She had climbed the heights of the "counters" and had seen things no other being could have possibly seen. There was no place within this realm she could be defeated! With a loud "Meeeerrrroooow" of a battle cry, she jogged on.

The bathroom being searched was cold and slippery, and she found nothing. Onward to the door! The edge of the realm and nothing. She forgot she had neglected the "Spare Room." She had battled there once. A furless with flames for hair had entered her realm uninvited, and she needed to terrify the peasant friend into submission as she had not shown the appropriate level of deference. She stalked with purpose, almost hoping to see this one again as she raised the spirits of the furless despite being absolutely annoying. She took a quick look and only saw her furless clacking away on their machines, typing poetry and sonnets in her name. She spoke to them and commanded them into action, but they were so ecstatically writing their devotions to her they merely crooned their love and carried on. In a huff of acceptance for their simple ways, she contemplated the realm and considered where else her foe could be hiding.

It hit her then. She sat with eyes round and glowing yellow like twin moons on a clear dark night.

The foe, more devious than she had ever imagined, dragged the simple Fool into the Space. The one space she loathed more than anywhere. It was darkly cramped and filled with machines of terrible design capable of destroying worlds, she was sure. She had never been able to figure out how the peasants used them or how they controlled them, which is why, aside from the delicious fish snacks, she kept them around. They seemed to be able to control these beasts of noise and chaos. Surely that was not where her enemy had stolen away the Fool! With a glance back at the simple-minded furless peasants, she steeled herself to face the worst.

In the center of Middle Hall lay a darkness filled with either haunting silence or terrifying sound beyond description. She steeled herself and called upon her fur mothers for strength. Despite the fear that was causing her fur to shape a ridge along her back in the style of battle and with a tail of such size and scope that no creature could take stock, she moved forward one paw at a time. Her stealth was as silent as a held breath, and she made no sound. She held her battle cry ready in the back of her throat as she approached the maw of the Space.

A slim crevice in the entrance to the Space only exposed darkness. Whatever death machines were held in this place were at the time silent, and the Queen knew she was blessed. Slinking forward so slowly, it was barely a movement, and she progressed to what could be her doom.

"Meeeeroooow, mroow meow!" The Fool leaped out of the depths bowling into her and calling loudly.

She fell back, cursing as he began babbling the details of the latest, most ridiculous of dreams to her. She raised up in an arch, laid back her ears flat, and hissed admonishment.

He looked at her stunned and asked if she wanted to climb the carpet tree and nap. She harrumphed and started to walk away. Indignant at the absolute audacity of this simpleton, she awaited him at the very top of the perch.

He followed in near jubilation and grinned at her, saying, "I love you, Shorty." To which the Queen replied, "Shut up," curled a paw around His head and licked his face before curling into a comma of balance with her Fool.

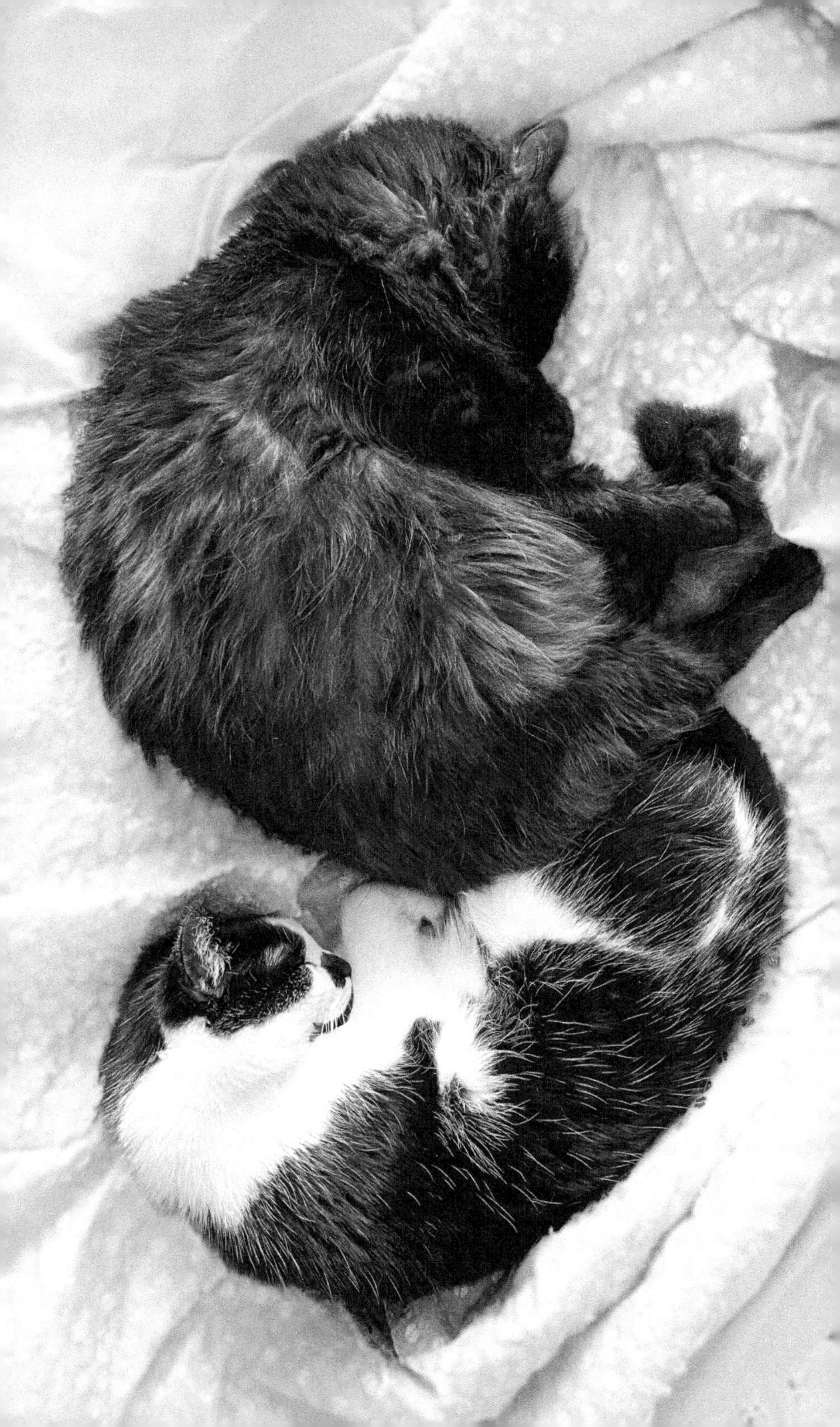

About the servant

My servant is a curious and dutiful ward. Many years ago he began documenting my grand and storied life and sharing it on the Tube of You to the great merriment of my citizens far and wide. With camera in one hand and poopsies scoopy in the other, he has been a trusted servant, more or less, ever since he rescued me from the dreadful Beast Barn as a young princess. Heavens, I was a sneezy, drippy mess; I'm certain that place gave me the plague. But he administered the remedies and nursed me back to fine form to build and expand my queendom. And it is good.

However, methinks my servant's gone a tad mad. For example, he seems to enjoy lifting heavy things off the floor and then putting them down again, and again and again, until breathless. Worse, he instructs others to do the same! If he spent as much time cleaning as he does lifting, perhaps the rats would stop moving in. Dimwit.

But a life of servitude to their ruler is one of great honour, so the servant is certainly grateful for that. See, dear reader, humans aren't entirely void of value. Do yourself a favour, and visit your nearest Beast Barn and rescue my kin to serve their every need. Or perhaps, pop by the castle and you can rescue the Simpleton from infecting mine eyes every day. Either way, you'll find purpose in what I'm certain is your otherwise dreary existence.

You're welcome.

Queen Shorty Shoshobeans

Printed in Great Britain
by Amazon